CLINICAL TRIALS AND DEATH

Book Eight: Fleming Investigations Cozy Mysteries

PATTI LARSEN

Cover design by Christina Gaudet
www.castlekeepcreations.com

Thanks, Kirstin!

ISBN-13: 978-1-989925-66-9

CHAPTER ONE

I WATCHED THE ORDERLY in blue scrubs and sneakers heading for our SUV, the wheelchair he pushed making me frown just a little. I was, after all, perfectly capable of walking, thank you. But when Crew opened my car door for me, I accepted the ride without argument, settling into the padded seat and allowing the smiling man to guide me up the walkway toward the glass entry of the Your Best Life Clinic, the beautifully manicured lawn and garden scape that made up the front face of the ultra-modern building complex a contrast to the glass and bright white boxiness.

"Welcome to Rhode Island," the cheery orderly said, his deep brown eyes as warm as his matching dark skin, teeth a flashing beacon in contrast. "We're so happy you're here, Mrs. Everett."

"Thank you," I said, doing my best to be demure and restrained. "I just hope you can help me."

"If anyone can," he assured me, pausing to open the main door for the chair via a push button that swung the heavy glass wide in a slow and silent motion, letting out cool, lavender-scented air as we passed through, "it's the fine doctors here at Your Best Life."

We'd see about that. What, you thought there was actually something wrong with me? To the contrary, thankfully, though I did my best to maintain that slightly concerned and reserved persona Crew built for me last night as we drove the last few miles to our destination.

"Mandy and Calvin Everett," he said. "I'm an accountant and you're a teacher." At least Mom's history at that job, along with her years as a principal in our hometown of Reading, Vermont, gave me enough insights I wouldn't have to do a lot of research. Though what my former FBI special agent turned sheriff turned private investigator husband knew about accounting I had no idea. Not that he was bad with money or anything, but I typically handled our finances out of habit after years of running my own bed and breakfast and now supervised the books for Fleming Investigations, our family PI business.

"That works," I told him while he unwound our story in that almost boyishly eager way of his when he took on a new case. I loved that about him, had only begun to see that joy in his job after he left the Reading Sheriff's Department and joined my dad and me at Fleming Investigations. "I'm just happy we finally get to work a case together."

"Me too." He'd reached across the console and squeezed my hand, held it the rest of the drive, the warm and comfortable silence between us a welcome shift from the awkward discomfort and unusual silence we'd battled since our fight a few days ago. We'd made up, of course, we had. I loved Crew, admired him for his tenacity and was happy he loved his job so much. But we'd been spending a lot of time apart thanks to the growing scope of our business, Fleming Investigations now with two offices—one at home in Reading and the other in Montpelier—along with travel cases Crew took on for a client who now owed both of us, it seemed, and called on my husband frequently for assistance.

In fact, Crew had turned down a job just yesterday for the mysterious and mega-wealthy Nelson Delamonte, to my surprise. In favor of taking this job. With me.

I loved my husband.

"Jill and Liz can handle it," he'd told me as we packed our suitcases into the car. "It'll be good for Nelson to have others in our organization to lean on. Besides, this is for the Aberstocks."

Right, did I fail to tell you that detail? My bad. We'd both had other plans, Crew and me, just forty-eight hours ago. Until a desperate call from Dr. Lloyd Aberstock—our favorite and not to be confused with his brother, Dr. Martin, and bane of my existence—had us both immediately agreeing to take on this case and make this journey out of state to Rhode Island and the Your Best Life Clinic.

No, not for Lloyd. As my orderly assistant slowed my progress across the white marble floor, pausing at the reception area, the cool, pale interior of the main entry soothing with that scent of lavender and piped-in piano music lilting just above audible levels, I reaffirmed why we were really here. Because Lloyd was worried about his wife, the darling Mrs. Claus to his Santa, Bernice Aberstock. She'd confided in me months ago she'd been diagnosed with cancer, and the prognosis, from what we knew, wasn't good. Which meant, if they needed us here? Heck, if they needed us at the North freaking Pole, I'd move heaven and earth to do whatever it took to fulfill the request.

"Mrs. Everett," the woman behind the desk smiled down at me, her perfect dark bob framing her olive cheeks, reminding me of Reading's mayor, Olivia Walker, and the mess I'd left behind a little too much for my liking. I hadn't spoken to Olivia since the O'Shea debacle over St. Patrick's Day, but I had a feeling a reckoning was coming and life in Reading wouldn't be the same after. A worry for another time as my greeter went on. "Welcome to the clinic. Is your husband with you?"

"Calvin is parking the car," I said, offering the fake ID Crew supplied (my husband had turned into quite the forger, it appeared) along with the paperwork I'd filled out on the drive.

"Excellent," she said, her silver nametag identifying her as Norma. "You're taking part in our fertility program, how exciting." Her kind and gentle smile was obviously meant to comfort me, increase my confidence, while I almost choked on the word fertility. Was this Crew's idea? Or Lloyd's? I managed to smile back, wondering if there was a message behind the choice of trials I'd been slotted into and trying not to read too much into it.

Hard, though, when I'd been thinking about babies lately.

"We're really hoping you can help," I said, biting my lower lip and feeling just the teensiest bit guilty (okay, a lot guilty) about lying to her. I had friends who couldn't have children, and it was no joking matter. Yes, I was undercover, okay, but I'd seen firsthand how devastating the inability to conceive could be, so taking it lightly was not on the agenda.

Then again, I realized as Norma signed off on my paperwork, how did I know for sure Crew and I could even have children? That thought had me chilled suddenly, hit me like a blow I wasn't expecting. There were no guarantees, after all. Maybe this was a good thing? An opportunity to find out if we could even conceive before we decided to move in that direction?

I was really getting ahead of myself, though my genuine reaction sold my performance, apparently, because not only did the orderly—his nametag now visible and identifying him as Henry—and Norma both sharing instant reactions of support, the woman circling to hand me the papers while he squeezed my shoulder with a gentle hand.

"Don't you worry even a little," Norma said, dark eyes crinkling around the corners as she smiled. "You're in excellent hands, Mandy. If anything can be done, it will be."

I nodded, surprised to find myself choked up, relieved when Crew joined us, taking Henry's place.

"You're all set, sweetheart?" He gently stroked my hair, bent and kissed my forehead. "She's been under such a strain." Crew's shift from confident, collected sexiness to this stranger wearing glasses, a button-up under a cardigan (where did he get a cardigan?) and a rather anxious and apologetic air about him had me staring a moment before I pulled myself together.

He was better at the subterfuge thing than I was. Almost too good, because I bought it like these strangers did, despite knowing him better than I knew myself. Or did I? For the first time, as I watched my husband in action, I realized there were sides of him—and was reminded he had a history before me—I had never seen before.

Well, being uncomfortable was a good thing, considering why we were there, so my own acting job passed, if for the wrong reasons.

"We totally understand," Norma was saying. "We're here to help. Henry, if you could take Mrs. Everett to her room and get her settled, Mr. Everett and I will finish up here." She beamed down at me.

"You'll be so happy you made the choice to come here, Mandy."

I didn't comment, my weak smile a byproduct of the spinning thoughts in my head, as the orderly spun me around and headed off at a brisk walk, past the main desk and toward a sunny hallway of glass and steel, the cheery sunshine doing nothing to lift my spirits.

I really needed to get a grip already.

CHAPTER TWO

THE SHORT WALK (RIDE) through the sunny hall ended in another doorway, this time a double swinging affair that felt a little more clinical, the far side with a spa-like atmosphere and that same music offering soothing (but landing in irritating, to be honest) accompaniment to the light, bright and cheerful colors of this part of the clinic. From the subtle gray of the floor to the pale yellow walls and pops of color on the occasional sofa, collection of chairs and even the doorways to what had to be rooms, I took note of how hard the designer had worked to ensure everything was not only perfectly placed and encouraged confidence and happiness, there were enough pictures of women holding babies, families playing (traditional and nontraditional alike) and adorable cherubs all on their own I felt my ovaries flutter.

Oh, dear.

My room stood at the far end, another set of white, swinging doors just past the red-painted joviality of the entry to my suite.

"What's past there?" Being nosy was going to be hard if I wanted to stay on the down-low, but it seemed an innocuous enough question and Henry didn't balk.

"That's the cancer wing," he said, still as cheery as ever while he palmed the button to automatically open my door, rolling me inside while he spoke. "We have one of the best clinical trials in the country going on right now."

So he said, but was the source of Lloyd Aberstock's concerned contact and supposed to be the focus of my attention. Ahem. Back to work, Fleming.

"How exciting," I said, one hand artfully pressed to my heart, wide eyes clearly getting the innocent point across.

Henry chuckled, locking my wheelchair and offering his own hand to assist me. I accepted the help, despite the fact I was in excellent physical condition, thank you. Clearly pampering the client was part of the service.

"It really is," he said. "Dr. Ian Linder is running the trial and we couldn't be happier to have him here." Was that a hitch in Henry's voice? A flicker of something not-so-happy? Whatever it was I thought

I saw, it vanished with another of the orderly's flashing smiles. "Now, you get settled and I'll make sure your husband knows where to find you." He unlocked the wheelchair before pausing one more moment. "You need anything, don't hesitate. The staff of Your Best Life is here for you, Mrs. Everett." With that, he turned and headed out at the same brisk stride, gone in a moment, leaving me to survey my new home.

There was certainly nothing hospitalish about it, though hints of clinical touches gave jarring reminders I wasn't in a luxury hotel room, from the metal handrail in the tiled shower stall and what looked like some kind of hoist system attached to the ceiling. And while there weren't rails on the bed or anything, the cupboard next to it contained a variety of medical machines I could identify as heart monitors, a CPAP mask and even what looked like a portable ultrasound.

The door opened while I closed the panel over the equipment, faintest sound and air displacement turning me to the entry, though the face I was expecting didn't appear, instead replaced by the familiar and dear one I'd come to miss in the last year or so since his wife's diagnosis. Dr. Lloyd Aberstock's perpetually cherubic and compassionate kindness had taken a beating in that time. He'd not only lost weight, his cheeks now seemed somewhat shrunken, bright blue eyes heavy-lidded and rolling, jolly walk reduced to slightly hunched and anxious instead. But the moment he saw me, his face lit up, the man he used to be making an appearance.

I surprised myself by hurrying to him with a low cry, hugging him tight, fighting tears and a thickening of my throat I could only banish with a deep, shaking breath and rough clearing of it. But when I pulled away, it was obvious to me I wasn't the only one in an emotional state, his blue eyes blinking rapidly and lower lip trembling as his smile lifted the gloom from his face and gave me hope my Dr. Aberstock wasn't gone just yet.

Hopefully to return completely in short order.

"Fiona," he said, squeezing my hand after letting me go, "thank you so much for coming." He waved off my attempt to speak, leading me to the sofa under the tall windows, seating me beside him and patting my knee before sitting back with a gusty sigh that sounded like he'd let out all the stress he'd been holding in one giant exhale. "I know, you must think I'm overreacting or overthinking, but I'm still grateful you and Crew could come." He turned as if only then realizing my husband was absent, smile fading just a little.

"He's finishing the paperwork," I said, Lloyd's expression flickering with relief and then a renewed happiness. "And no, we don't think anything of the sort." When his phone call outlined his concerns about the trial—the very one I'd just talked to Henry about, in fact—and Bernice's participation, Crew and I both immediately took the job (pro bono, though the Aberstocks would fight us on it, naturally, but that was for later) and dug into research the moment we accepted. "From what we uncovered, clinical trials like this one can be fraught with issues, so you have every right to be worried." While most trials were on the up-and-up, there was enough evidence of tampering in this particular industry—oh, and it was big business, make no mistake—it was hardly a reach for Lloyd to be concerned.

He seemed even more relieved, shaking his head, full, white beard brushing the collar of his t-shirt under his plaid button-up. "It's Bernie," he whispered, voice low and cracking. I held quiet and let him gather himself, holding still and giving him space until he cleared his own throat and flickered that smile again. "How are things at home?"

He didn't want to get into that with me. "Let's focus on the case," I said. Because the giant mess that was the remains of the cutest town in America would only stress him out, I had no doubt, and he needed to focus on Bernice. "She's more important right now." More important than the fact almost every small business in our hometown was now shuttered and under investigation thanks to the infiltration and overtaking of the O'Shea crime family, with only a handful, like French's Handmade Bakery and The Iris, still operating. It might have only been just past the middle of March and not quite yet the spring shoulder season, but summer was fast approaching and with Reading on the edge of bankruptcy thanks to criminal interference, even Olivia's ambitions might not be enough to pull us up and out of hardship in time to salvage the tourist season.

I highly doubted visitors were interested in our kind of ghost town.

And without a sheriff's department, we were at the mercy of the state police, replacement staff as yet unhired, a new sheriff likely in the offing if Olivia had her way. But without the funds to hire, we instead had Officers Brown and Williams patrolling our streets, with the occasional stop-in visit from BCI Detective Rowan Mallory to keep things official.

"I read Pamela's expose," Lloyd said then, meaning the cat was already not just out of the bag, it was screeching its unhappiness at being shoved into one in the first place.

"You know Pamela," I said, a weak attempt to deflect. "She's so hard-hitting sometimes she forgets there are people on the other end of her story." The former *Boston Globe* investigative reporter turned managing editor and writer for the *Reading Reader Gazette* hadn't pulled a single punch, even calling out Eve O'Shea and my own godfather, Malcolm Murray, for turning state's evidence against the Goth girl's family. Her feature had been picked up by major newspapers around the country, so I wasn't surprised he'd heard the gorier details, if out of full context, though Lloyd Aberstock was never one to leap to conclusions or judge others without his own extensive investigation into matters.

"Our dear little town is once again the center of attention," he said, voice low and sad, "but not for reasons Olivia would like, I dare say." He sighed again, shrugged. "Things will be what they are. You and I, my dear Fiona, have done our best by Reading all these years. As have your father and mother, your husband and yes, even Pamela Shard." I nodded. "I can only hope there's a Reading to go home to when all of this is over."

I caught my breath, couldn't help it. "Over?" As in…

His blue eyes met mine, serious and quiet. "I need you and Crew to find out if the trial is valid or not," he said, voice vibrating with anxiety despite his level look. "Because if it's not, if it's all a lie…" he looked away, swallowed. "If I let Martin talk me into this trial and it's a fraud, Fee, when I could have enrolled Bernice in another, I'll never forgive myself."

Or him, I assumed, though it wasn't spoken. The fact Lloyd and his brother had been estranged for over thirty years, only coming together again thanks to Bernice and her illness—and a quick job on my part as requested by Lloyd's wife—meant there was already a strain on their relationship dating back decades. A strain I'd never learned the history behind, as it turned out. But regardless, I had no doubt if something did happen to Bernice, if this trial she was in ended badly, my Dr. Aberstock wouldn't be in the most forgiving frame of mind.

And I wouldn't blame him even a little bit.

"Have you spoken to Robert?" I blinked at Lloyd when he asked that question, surprised by it, taken off guard. My hateful cousin, former sheriff and pain-in-my-butt Robert Carlisle had managed to escape prosecution for any role he might have played in both the Patterson affair and the O'Shea debacle, by giving over evidence of value to the state's attorney's office. Meanwhile, the other half of Rosebert was on her way to prison for life, at least, so I could be thankful for that blessing. Honestly, despite Reading's bad way at the moment, my town was finally free and for the first time in a very long time, so blessings were counted daily.

But why was Lloyd thinking about Robert at a time like this? "I saw him once since the O'Sheas were arrested," I said, trying not to think about the warehouse raid, about my cousin's shift in character, my long-held dislike (and downright hatred at times, I admit it, because I'm a bigger person than him, thanks) challenged by unexpected compassion. Robert had seemed deflated, his normal cock-of-the-walk strutting arrogance lost, that horrible 70s pornstache of his overgrown, shoulders hunched, potbelly reduced for the first time in years, spindly legs and round center making him appear almost spider-like, ungainly. Made me wonder why he even stayed in Reading, lingering despite himself, perhaps, a shadow of the (barely a) man he was.

"Fee," Lloyd said then, leaning toward me, intensity in his eyes, "please don't take this the wrong way, but your cousin is a ticking timebomb and if something isn't done, I fear he might do something we'll all regret."

CHAPTER THREE

I WAS, NATURALLY, ABOUT to ask him just what he was talking about when the door opened, and Crew walked in. My husband took one look at my guest and grinned, sweeping the horn-rimmed glasses from his face, his accountant's hunch disappearing as Crew Turner took over from Calvin Everett. He strode forward with one hand out, Lloyd standing to shake it, though the pair ended up in a bearhug when the doctor tugged on my husband and drew him closer.

"Thank you," our friend said. "This means the world to me."

"John had to fight me over the assignment," Crew said, nodding to me. I didn't know that, hadn't heard the pair talked it over. "He wanted to come, but since you signed Fee up in the fertility clinic, I argued her husband was a better option than her dad." Um, yeah. Wait, what?

"What is that about anyway?" I poked Lloyd as the doctor sat again, Crew perching next to him, the twinkle back in my friend's eyes as my Dr. Aberstock—had been, was and always would be, so take that, Martin Poserstock—shrugged and winked at my husband.

"I doubt you have anything to worry about," Lloyd said as he patted my knee with his familiar and kind smile back to a hundred watts and making me feel better. "I thought it a good cover story, considering your recent marriage. And, what an excellent opportunity for the two of you, really. Since you're here anyway and I may have dragged you across two states for a wild goose chase." Lloyd's energy ebbed again, his mind clearly on Bernice before he brightened once more. "Since your mother and father could only have you, I thought we'd take care of two issues with one visit." I almost grunted in surprise. Hang on, what did he just say? I sat back with a vague feeling of selfishness and guilt rising. I'd never asked Mom and Dad why I was an only child. I'd always just assumed they'd found perfection (snort) and decided to stop at me. The idea my mother and father couldn't have more kids never crossed my mind. And had me worrying all over again despite Lloyd's assurances.

Meanwhile, he was clearly assessing my mental state, because he leaned in and tweaked the lobe of my ear, just like he used to do when I was little and he was my GP, not Reading's ME.

"Young lady," he said, his old self fully surfacing at last, the man I adored my whole life smiling at me in that jovial good humor that was irresistible and banished all concerns, "it was either that or pretend you had cancer. I assume you had no desire to shave that glorious red hair of yours?" My hands instantly went to my head (vanity, thy name was Fiona Fleming) while Crew let out a little bark of laughter even as he blanched. I wasn't the only one attached to my thick, auburn locks, was I? Lloyd let out his own chuckle. "Exactly," he said. "This clinic focuses on reproduction and death. I have no choice in the matter right now, and neither does my dear Bernice. I couldn't bear to put you in that position too. So, for you, my dear Fee, Crew, my boy, I chose life."

Was he trying to make me bawl like a baby? I wasn't about to argue with him or his logic, however.

"Why don't you tell us why we're really here." Leave it to Crew to help us focus. "We got the gist from your call, but we'd love more details."

Lloyd had sobered as well, though the kind and lovely man I knew remained, that haunted shell of Dr. Aberstock gone with our arrival, thank goodness. I planned to do everything in my power to ensure he never came back.

"Martin is an old friend of Ian Linder," Lloyd said, hands clasping in his lap, cheeks pink though his earlier anxiety seemed to have disappeared or had at least been softened enough he wasn't so visibly choked by it. "It's the reason Bernice was accepted into the trial." It couldn't have been easy, since trusting his brother meant putting his wife's life in that same man's hands. "I thought everything was fine. Bernice has been doing very well." He sounded optimistic briefly, but his face fell as he went on. "Until an FDA investigator showed up."

"It could be just a routine check-in?" I knew better than to try to reassure him but couldn't help myself. Still, my research told me such inquiries and visits were common when it came to ongoing trials. The FDA was careful around tests like this one, to make sure the public was protected. And in cases of cancer trials, caution was even more encouraged because the potential for harm—and healing—was so high.

Lloyd nodded, though his troubled expression said there was more to it. "She's been here for a week," he said. "That's not normal, Fee. And no one will explain why she's here."

Yeah, that didn't sound good. "You said Bernice is improving?" Unlike the previous topic, this one had an excellent ring to it.

My friend hesitated but sighed as he nodded one more time, almost like he fought agreement. "She seems to be," he said. "In fact, truth be told, she's the best she's been in months." Desperate hope surfaced before retreating. "But it could simply be a rally, for all I know. I've been cut out of the process, and I don't like it one bit."

"You're a doctor," I said.

"But not on the research team," he told me. "And the drug trial is proprietary, so I'm not privy to any information aside from what a layperson would know about the treatment."

"Is this a blind trial, Lloyd?" Crew frowned as his agile mind worked over the case, an excellent question.

"No," our doctor friend said, "not in this instance. They are in the final stage of testing. Which means everyone on the trial is receiving the drug, so if it is working, it's not a placebo effect, at least." He ran both hands through his white hair, in need of a haircut for the first time since I'd known him, his normally tidy and trimmed appearance somewhat abandoned in the face of what he endured. "I want to believe," he said then, barely above a whisper. "And maybe I'm wasting all of our time. Maybe she really is getting better, and the drug is working. I just need to know one way or the other and no one here will tell me anything." His frustration came through again, both hands balling into round fists on his thighs. "I thought I was prepared already. To lose her." My heart broke for him as he squared his shoulders. "Then this hope surfaced, hope I hadn't felt since her diagnosis." I couldn't even imagine and glanced up at Crew, saw his face tighten, knew he had to be thinking about his first wife. Michele had died of breast cancer, and he'd lost her mother, Carol, a year and a half ago. My darling husband was well aware of the weight and repercussions of this horrible disease, more than I was. Lloyd looked up in a rush, patting Crew's knee as his hands unclenched. "I'm sorry, my boy," he said. "I know this is hitting close to home."

So kind of him to think of Crew in that moment of hurt. It was Lloyd Aberstock down to the ground and a big part of the reason we all adored him. My husband shook his head, blue eyes lifting to me as he spoke.

"I've lost to cancer," he said, "but I found love again, Lloyd. Life has to go on."

Our doctor friend hitched his breath, nodded. "I need to know one way or the other," he said. "That's all. I just need to know."

Fair enough. "We'll do everything we can," I said, fighting more tears, wanting to hug him even as he stood, offering me his hand while he helped me to my feet in the most gentlemanly way.

"I know you will," Lloyd said, hugging me before shaking Crew's hand. "Don't worry about your cover story. I'll tell Bernice you're here on a case and to pretend that we're old friends from elsewhere."

That helped a lot. "We'll dig in," I said, following him to the door, Crew at my side. "And keep you posted."

"I'll walk you out." Crew left with Lloyd, catching my gaze on the way through the door, the old sorrow I used to see in him back for a moment. The sorrow he carried with him the first few years I knew him, the hurt that was Michelle. And then, his eyes lit up and he smiled, and I knew everything was going to be all right, no matter what.

Because he was right. Life went on and we were lucky enough to have found love in it.

I barely had time to process my emotions when the door opened again, and a perky blonde whirlwind entered. She stopped abruptly at the sight of us, eyes widening in surprise, O forming from her perfect pink lips. But before I could recover and ask her what she was doing barging in like she had, she beamed at me from her barely five-foot height, hazel gaze sparkling when she extended her hands in a rush of enthusiasm.

"You're here!" She grasped me in a firm grip. "I'm so excited you made it safe and sound." Well, that was sweet of her, right? "Mrs. Everett," she gushed, "I'm Brooke Poplar, one of the nurses in charge of your care. Let's get you pregnant!"

CHAPTER FOUR

NOW, I WAS WELL aware she couldn't possibly have meant it the way it came out, but I still giggled like a teenage girl at the implication while Brooke blushed and laughed herself, eyes widening as she snorted along with me before we both regained our composure.

"You're adorable," she said. "And you know what I meant."

"I do," I said, grinning. "Still funny, though."

"I'm glad you can laugh about it." She offered one hand, her sweet expression kind and compassionate, flush of amusement fading from her cheeks. "I promise, we'll do everything we can to make sure you have all the information you need on how to proceed." She giggled again, though not as freely. "I'm sure you and your husband have that part handled." I winked and she laughed one more time. "When biology doesn't behave the way you want it to, even when *you're* not behaving," her sly smile had me blushing this time, "that's where we come in." She squeezed my fingers before releasing me, beaming expression warming the room as much as the sun coming in the tall windows. "I'm on the floor the next few days, so if you need anything at all, please don't hesitate, okay?"

I nodded. "Thanks, Brooke," I said, that twinge of guilt over lying about my real reason for being there waking once more. I squashed it firmly, since for all I knew I really did need their services (heaven forbid) and chose to focus on the case. "I have a friend here," I said then. "She and her husband recommended the clinic to my husband and me. Bernice Aberstock?"

Brooke's eyes told me what her words didn't, flicker of worry there enough to concern me. "Dear Bernice and Lloyd," she said, sounding chipper enough as she fixed me with a more professional smile than before. "Of course, you'll want to visit."

"Is that all right?" I nodded toward the door. "Henry said the cancer wing was on the other side of the doors in the hall."

Brooke took my hand again and led me out into the main corridor, pointing toward the very doors I'd mentioned. "Through there, the third on your right. Bernice is such a darling, I know she'll be delighted to see an old friend."

"How is she?" I blurted the question before I could stop myself, even as the young nurse tilted her head, with a firm finger shake in my direction though she continued to smile.

"I'm not allowed to divulge personal information," she said. Then leaned in with that sneaky grin again. "That doesn't mean you can't go ask her yourself, though, does it?"

I liked her way of thinking. "Thank you," I said.

"I'll see you in a little bit for your first appointment," Brooke said, waving as she strode off on her short legs at a surprisingly rapid speed, vanishing around the corner far faster than I could have managed. Leaving me to turn and push through the swinging door toward the reason I was here, my own feet feeling leaden as they plodded in slow motion over the polished floor.

Of course, I wanted to see Bernice. I hadn't spoken to her in months, Lloyd's protectiveness and obvious goal to find a cure for her illness meaning they'd both been absent from Reading since she'd been diagnosed. I adored both her and her husband so much, but.

I'll admit it. I was afraid to see her. What if I couldn't keep it together? There was an excellent chance she looked like, well, death. I'd never faced that before. Sure, I'd seen dead bodies aplenty, but someone on the verge of death? Someone I loved? That got me started on worrying about Mom and Dad. They weren't getting any younger, were they? And Petunia, my darling pug, safely at home with my parents and being pampered, no doubt. She'd been slowing down in recent months, had been through so much, the old dear. I hadn't been close to Grandmother Iris when she passed, so I'd never really lost anyone near and dear to me before. How would I handle it when my dog—my daily companion and overlady—left me?

How would I survive without her?

I stopped abruptly, eyes burning, the world wavering behind a layer of moisture that threatened to spill over and take me down. What the actual...? Something was wrong with me, clearly, that I'd gone from normal woman to standing on the brink basket case in barely a few feet of corridor. Even in that state, I realized I couldn't just lose my crap in the quiet of the hallway. I needed somewhere to pull myself together from this weird, unnerving and uncomfortable surge of feeling that tried to knock me off my feet.

As I spun to go back to my room, my gaze passed a door, the silver label marking it as storage. Without further thought, the sound of someone approaching driving me to hide rather than share, I ducked through the doorway and into the dark and silent room beyond.

There was just enough light coming through at the threshold I navigated without running into anything, the space filled with rows of metal racks stacked with linens and supplies. Heart pounding, barely able to breathe, I strode all the way to the back and down one side, tucking myself into the back corner with the racks hiding my presence before I bent in half, hands on my knees, and let out a few silent sobs through my open mouth.

I hadn't expected to feel this emotional. I hadn't even seen Bernice yet, after all. Anticipation had always been my downfall, making my mind turn and twist into horrible possibilities that could have been easily relieved by a confrontation with truth. But this? This was a new realm and level of holy hecking feck that had me floored.

Had I finally lost it? No, come on now, Fee. Deep breath, woman, and stop leaping to worst-case scenarios already. Logic was my friend in times like this, so I called up what little I had access to and forced my emotions to submit to the rational.

I suppose it was a mix of worry for her, new worry I hadn't considered about my own future as a mother (or not) tied to the recent fight with Crew that bundled together into the kind of perfect feeling storm that had me hunched over in a storage closet, panting near-hysterical tears into the silent space while the world went on without me.

Look, I'm a redhead. I get we're emotional creatures, prone to temper and torment. But this was the first time in a long time I'd crumpled, and it scared me, really scared me. What if Bernice died? What if Lloyd left Reading forever? What if Petunia passed when I was here, and she died without me there? What if Crew and I fought again, and again, and couldn't get past fighting?

What if I couldn't have kids?

Oh. Okay. Yeah. There it was, then. The real root of it after all.

Argh.

Understanding brought clarity and calm, both hands rising to wipe at the tears, my shoulders relaxing, body aquiver with extra adrenaline while I shook my head at myself. Ridiculous, and yet, obviously a necessary moment of panic I'd been suppressing. Because it wasn't that I'd been trying to get pregnant or anything, right?

But I hadn't exactly *not* been trying if you know what I mean. If it happened, great, if not… I guess I was facing if not, wasn't I? Far more powerfully and out of the blue than I'd planned. No wonder it hit me so hard.

Oh, Fee.

At least now that I'd admitted to myself there might be a problem after all, I could do something about it. Funny how we convince ourselves nothing is wrong while letting fear and anxiety fester inside unchecked and unnoticed until something like my present breakdown moment happened. Fortunately for me, I got to lose it alone in a dark closet where I could both dissolve into a puddle of goo and collect myself while admitting my real concern without any public displays of overly emotional hysteria. So that was a win, right?

I finally caught my breath, the last of my tears wiped free on the cuffs of my shirt, heart rate slowed to more normal, and determination to confront my real fear and ask questions about possible outcomes replacing the now identifiable ache of worry my mind had been nurturing without my consent.

Even as I made the choice to exit and go find Crew, tell him about my fear, expose it to the open air as the ridiculous angst it was, the door to the storage room opened and someone entered.

I froze in place, not sure what to do, catching my breath. Now, it wasn't like I'd done anything wrong. But the fact my first instinct, when confronted with the unknown, was to go still and silent was kind of telling, don't you think? I guess I'd been in too many situations over the years where threat was more common than the contrary had me reacting instead of acting.

That's why, the moment the door opened again, and a second person entered, I was in the perfect position to eavesdrop on the two men who now hissed in angry voices at one another.

CHAPTER FIVE

I S IT WRONG I was grateful for the distraction? Probably, but I took the interruption as a sign and eased forward while the two male voices rose a little in volume, more than enough for me to make them out audibly.

"You can't just cut me out, Ian," the first man was saying with a faint Latino accent.

"I can," the other man said, voice cold and harsh. "And I am. It's already done, Che. Live with it."

I heard a scuffle, peeked around the corner of the rack in time to see the two shadows—my eyes adjusted enough to make out white lab coats—in a physical struggle as one tried to restrain the other briefly.

"Enough," the one named Ian said as the shapes

separated, the taller and leaner of the two staggering back, the shorter, rounder raising one arm between them. "I warned you this would happen if you didn't back me up. You've outlived your usefulness on the trial, Che. Go back to your new research and leave curing cancer to those of us who have the nerve for it." The shorter man then jerked the door open, almost hitting the taller with it as he squeezed out and slammed it behind him.

The man identified as Che swore in Spanish, and while I wasn't fluent in that language by any means, I understood a few of the expletives and the context well enough. I huddled, heart pounding all over again, as he spun and grasped something on one of the shelves, hurtling it back toward me, forcing me to duck as a bin crashed into the wall, lid flying off, items once held within scattering everywhere. I just managed to shield my face and keep from squeaking out a protest before he stormed out of the room himself, one more slam ending in quiet.

Well, almost quiet, since my anxious panting now sounded so loud in my ears, I was sure they could hear me at the front desk. It took me a bit to gather myself and creep to the door, taking a fast look through the crack I made before I bolted, head down, heading for Bernice's door.

Maybe I should have just gone back to my own room at that point, but I wasn't thinking straight and all I could think of was to get to my goal. Which meant as I arrived at the indicated entry, I simply pushed it open and hurried inside, not bothering to knock or warn the occupant of my arrival.

Not that it mattered. I stumbled to a halt just across the threshold, the door swinging shut behind me, as none other than Bernice Aberstock looked up from her sofa—the layout of her room matching mine perfectly if the décor palate had been swapped from yellow to green—and let out a happy chirp of surprise.

"Fee!" She stood immediately, hurrying to my side, hugging me with such strength and enthusiasm I sagged into her rather than the other way around. When I pushed her back, reassuring myself what I'd seen and experienced was real and not my imagination, studying her with wide eyes, she laughed, her old and familiar laugh that made me tear up all over again. "I'm fine," she said, patting both of my cheeks with her hands, light in her pale blue eyes, skin warm and pink and cheeks plump with good health. In fact, if it wasn't for the pink and purple patterned scarf she wore tied around her head, and her lack of eyelashes and eyebrows, I honestly wouldn't have known she'd been ill enough to require the kind of chemo that ended in hairlessness. "My dear, you look a fright." Her joy at my arrival had turned to concern as she led me to the sofa to sit next to her. "Are you all right?"

No way was I dumping what I'd just been through on the woman I'd come to rescue. Oh, make no mistake, that's why I was here and there were no its, buts or ands about it. My inability to do anything to help her since she'd confided in me had obviously been weighing on me as much as everything else. Seeing her healthy deflated that self-centered sense of purpose to the point I was positive I'd burst into tears no matter how hard I tried not to.

"I'm just so happy to see you," I said, managing to gasp that out without sobbing like a lunatic. "You look wonderful." Was that the wrong thing to say to someone with cancer?

Bernice beamed back at me, squeezing my hands. "Fiona, I feel fantastic," she gushed. "This trial Lloyd has me in is a miracle, I swear. It's been touch and go, dear." She nodded slowly, lower lip quivering while my compassion for her took another giant leap and I finally felt like I could help if only to slip one arm around her shoulders and hug her while she went on. "This has been a horrible ordeal, and I don't recommend it."

"I'll keep that in mind," I whispered through a tight throat. "Bernice does not recommend cancer, 1 out of 10 stars."

She giggled. "Exactly." A giant sigh seemed to free her from the moment of anxiety and helped me, too, enough I let her go and managed to smile back at her joyfully returned expression. "It's so lovely of you to visit, Fee, but." She frowned a little then, more confused than anything, glancing at the door. "Why are you here?"

Oops. So, Lloyd hadn't told her anything, huh? Which meant I could either tell her the truth or maintain the cover we'd created. And, in a horrible moment of weakness, I chose the latter.

"The fertility clinic," I blurted.

Bernice's eyes lit up like never before, huge O of her pink painted lips turning to a giant smile as she hugged me tight, rocking me, fingers practically digging into my arms. "Fiona Marie Fleming," she whispered. "How wonderful for both of you."

I was a terrible, terrible friend. "Your trial is going well, then?" Of course, it was. I deflected from her excitement, though she didn't seem to mind, clapping her hands in front of her as she eye-rolled her delight.

"Dr. Linder is amazing," she said. "Fee, I'll tell you honestly, there was a time I wasn't sure if I would make it." She sighed another small, contented sigh. "But this trial has given me so much hope. Whatever the outcome, even if I only get to feel this well for now, I'm so grateful."

Just like Bernice to wrap the experience in a silver lining. I didn't get to congratulate her, not when the door to her room opened and Lloyd walked through, Crew at his back. She rose to hug her husband and then mine, lips pressing to Crew's cheek a moment.

"Congratulations, dear," she said to him as his blue eyes lifted to mine. "You two are going to make the most beautiful babies." She clasped her hands under her chin, looking back and forth between us while her husband smiled his own indulgence. "My own dear Lloyd and I were never blessed with children of our own." I knew that, flinched again with the guilt of this whole situation. "I can't wait to dote on your gorgeous little ones." She hesitated then, looking back and forth between us as if making a connection she hadn't before. "I'm sorry, kids. I didn't even... are you having trouble?"

She was not carrying that worry around in her head for another second. "Not at all," my amazing husband said instantly. "In fact, we're just here to make sure everything is okay before we start our family." He met my eyes again, his utter authenticity so complete and believable that I actually felt my stomach flutter with anxiety all over again. I had no idea he was such a good liar. "Right, sweetheart?"

I bobbed a nod, then shook my head. "We're here on a case," I said, ruining everything.

Bernice's surprise flashed across her face. "Oh, dear," she said.

If my husband could have glared me into the ground, I know he would have, though Lloyd looked embarrassed when his wife turned to him, rather than angry.

"Tell me this isn't about me," she said, admonishment just below chastising.

"The FDA investigator," he said.

"You're overreacting," she said. "I spoke to Lauren myself. She reassured me everything is fine."

"Ms. Sigler isn't allowed to tell you anything other than that," Lloyd said, visibly flustered.

They didn't speak again for another long moment, simply staring at one another like a pair of people who had been together for so many years words were no longer necessary to get a point across. Until Lloyd sighed and reached for her, and they hugged it out.

"They're just making sure everything is okay," he said.

Bernice nodded against her husband's chest, but when she released him, she fixed first me and then Crew with a wry smile. "You two," she said, "are dear friends and I know we've been keeping to ourselves. I'm so grateful you came to help, I really am. I know Lloyd has been worried even though I'm feeling so much better. So, do what you came to do and know I adore you both for it."

I'd have been furious to find out we'd been sneaking around behind her back. Not Bernice Aberstock. The world didn't deserve women like her.

The door swung open, the small, blonde nurse I'd already met sweeping inside. I guess I wasn't the only one who didn't knock around here. Brooke Poplar smiled at the Aberstocks, then at Crew and me, perky jaunt to her high pony swinging it to the side.

"I love it when friends come together," she chirped. "Nice reunion?"

We didn't get to respond because she wasn't the only visitor. Just as she finished speaking, the door swung inward one more time, and a short, roundish man in a white lab coat, his round glasses sparkling in the light and gruff expression about as no-nonsense as I'd ever seen, strode in. Took one look at the lot of us and grunted.

"Mrs. Aberstock," he said in a voice I recognized as one of the men who'd argued in the closet.

"Dr. Linder," she said with a smile. "My

friends—"

"Were going," he snapped. "We have an exam scheduled." Ian Linder didn't even look our way. "Out. Now."

Wow. Talk about lack of bedside manner. But Bernice didn't seem put off and despite Lloyd's visible irritation at the other doctor's attitude, I figured she was in good hands. Which had me turning toward the exit despite rankling against the abrupt dismissal. Only to catch the anxious and almost panicked look on Brooke's face.

Well now. He might have been mean to me, but what did he have on her?

CHAPTER SIX

"I HAD SOME QUESTIONS about the efficacy—" Lloyd's attempt to speak up ended abruptly as Dr. Ian Linder jerked his thumb over one shoulder, this battle clearly not a first-time thing.

"And what," Linder said while the door opened a third time and a tall, handsome man entered, skin tone and dark eyes making him Latino and encouraging my mind to leap to an obvious conclusion this must be Che, "exactly, would a medical examiner," Linder fixed Lloyd with a derisive stare that would have garnered a smackdown if he aimed it at me, thank you very much, "and a general practitioner," oh no, he did *not* just dis my favorite doctor on the planet, "know about the efficacy," seriously, could he dip any lower with his disdain? I think not, "in a drug trial for cancer research?"

They glared at one another while the tall doctor strode in, kind smile a far cry from the bitter challenge on his counterpart's face.

"Dr. Aberstock," the newcomer said in a kind tone that disarmed the room somewhat, "Mrs. Aberstock."

"Dr. Mantegna," Lloyd said, ruffled but holding it together.

"I told you like I told your brother," Ian Linder snapped as if the other doctor hadn't spoken, "if you refuse to mind your own business you will be asked to leave." He jabbed an index finger at Bernice. "Both of you. And considering your wife's excellent progress, that would be a shame."

Lloyd's face flushed deep red, my jaw jumping at the connotation of this conversation. Would he really eject a woman with terminal cancer from a program that might be saving her life because he was an arrogant asshat without any social skills whatsoever and an ego the size of a dump truck?

Whatever my Dr. Aberstock was about to say in response died instead of his wife, because that lovely lady, unfazed and smiling, even, nodded to her husband before patting Dr. Linder's raised hand.

"He'll behave, Ian," she said in that sweet tone of hers. "They all will." Her eyes met mine, a plea there.

Oh, dear.

Linder appeared disarmed by her attitude, clearing his throat and adjusting his tie a moment before he nodded once in abrupt acceptance of her assurance. "Shall we, Mrs. Aberstock?"

She followed him out of the room, kissing my cheek on the way by with a whispered, "thank you," before disappearing through the door. I did note Brooke kept her head down and avoided making eye contact with Dr. Linder, though that grumpy so-and-so took a moment to flash her a disapproving stare that had me wondering all over again what it was he didn't like about her. Then again, the man was clearly a piece of work, so as far as I was concerned the kindly young nurse could do no wrong and the doctor was being a jerkface for the sake of jerkfacing.

So, there.

"You'll forgive my colleague's abruptness." Dr. Che Mantegna's smile widened on his handsome face, hand gripping mine as he shook it, then Crew's, before turning to Lloyd who spluttered a moment but couldn't seem to pull together the words he wanted. Che's hand landed on the smaller man's shoulder, sympathy on his face. "Ian might not be good with people," he said, "but he's an excellent researcher." Wait, what was that crossing the doctor's expression even as he spoke the words. Doubt? Or maybe it was just the fact the pair had fought not so long ago. Which meant either Dr. Mantegna was here out of turn, or they'd made up.

Turned out it was the latter as he then returned his attention to us. "You must be the Everett's," he said. "I'm Dr. Che Mantegna. I'll be supervising your testing during your stay with us."

Lloyd seemed instantly concerned, frowning at the taller doctor. "But Bernice's trial...?"

"I've been asked to resume my specialty," Che said in a smooth and hearty tone that covered his irritation. Trust me, I caught the undercurrent of it, but I was in the know, right? Neither Lloyd nor Crew seemed to have registered the tall doctor's annoyance. "Bernice is in great hands, and I have happy couples to care for." He flashed me a smile. "Now, let's get you two over to our clinic and start those tests, shall we? I'd like to see a bouncing baby Everett in your future." He nodded to Brooke who seemed shaken but managed to smile back, brave face on. "If you could escort the Everetts to the clinic, Brooke, I have one last thing to look into." He exited then, leaving the nurse to gesture to the door, her sparkle gone.

I blamed Dr. Linder. You better believe it.

"We'll be one moment," Crew said, smiling at Brooke. She shrugged and left after he continued to stare in that dismissive way of his, leaving the three of us alone.

"I'm sorry about that," Lloyd said immediately, both hands clutching together as he turned to pace. "Linder won't tell me anything and he keeps threatening to eject Bernice if I don't stay out of his research." He stopped suddenly, panic rising in his eyes, licking his lips while his whole body stiffened. "I just want this to work. I want it to be real."

I hurried to him, hugged him. "So do we," I said.

"I'll look into the FDA issue," Crew said, while I

felt myself frown a little. Oh, he would, would he? Not we? Then crushed the surge of resentment at his wording, knowing I was jumping to overreaction unnecessarily thanks to my own elevated emotional state. Look at me being all adult and understanding and such.

"I just wish I knew if her being here was actually cause for alarm or if I'm making a mountain out of a molehill." Lloyd hugged me back before letting me go. "I'm sorry to put you in this position. I meant to tell Bernice you were coming but I didn't know how. I knew she'd be upset with me."

"Fee took care of that," Crew said, so dismissively I actually stared at him with a sizzling hit of irritation tracing a line in the sand between us. "We need you to focus on Bernice and leave the job you asked us to do to us. Okay?"

Lloyd nodded, squeezing my hand, faint smile returning. "I knew reaching out to you was the right choice, Fee," he said, blinking too fast again while I did in return. "I'm so sorry about Martin."

That was unexpected and not something he needed to be thinking about at the moment. "Your brother is a professional," I said. "And our relationship is not your problem."

"He's been horrible," Lloyd said. "To you, to Penny Keene." The new ME assistant and my friend had been having her conflicts with my Dr. Aberstock's brother, that much was true, but she was a big girl and I'd seen her handle herself not just competently, but with real enthusiasm for her job.

The fact our Dr. Aberstock had been her mentor and was the reason she'd moved to Reading to take the ME assistant job in the first place? All the more reason for me to like her and side with her, even if I wasn't ready to regardless. Honestly, Penny could have been a total ass and I would have liked her more than Martin. No grudges or anything. "I should never have let Bernice talk me into reconnecting."

And that fired up the old curiosity engine like nothing else. But before I could ask Lloyd point-blank—yeah, that would have happened, believe it—about his reasons for cutting off his brother for so long, Crew interrupted.

"Get some rest," he said, reaching out and taking my arm, tugging me away from Lloyd while I again frowned at my husband's attitude. "We'll dig around and keep you in the loop. Don't worry," he said as he practically dragged me to the door, "we've got this."

And then we were out in the hallway, Brooke down the corridor a bit talking to Henry and out of the way and earshot Crew obviously thought it safe to speak his mind.

Which he did, hissing in my ear, while my pulse pounded, and the old redheaded temper fired up for real.

"Bernice didn't need to know," he said. "Follow my lead from now on." With that, Crew turned and walked away, adopting his hunched-shouldered persona again, glasses returned to his face, ingratiating tone smothering the now smiling Brooke Poplar while I bit back a response that my darling husband wouldn't have liked if he'd heard it out loud.

Didn't keep me from saying it in my head. Follow his lead? What was I, his subordinate or something? He'd clearly forgotten I was co-owner with Dad of Fleming Investigations. Fleming. *Not* Turner. He worked for *me*.

Snarl, growl, *argh*.

And as I let that heated anger simmer, I made a choice he'd have hated. To take a peek into Martin Aberstock at long last, if only to spite my husband.

CHAPTER SEVEN

WHILE THE REST OF the clinic might have looked like an attempt at a soothing resort, the clinic itself had that professional, sterile feel I'd been expecting. And though it should have felt comforting, perhaps, that Your Best Life Clinic took this part of the process seriously without the frilly bells and whistles I'd seen so far, it only made things worse. Not their fault entirely, however. And surely, I wasn't the only person in the world who felt this way, unnerved and vulnerable as I sat on a traditional exam table in what amounted to a high-end hospital gown (that tied in the front like a robe, at least) waiting on the doctor to arrive for our chat. I found myself squirming and wriggling and trying to shake off the awkward and unhappy physical sensation that being in a physician's office often stirred in me, all while trying to balance out the newly discovered discomfort I'd uncovered when it came to the topic I was about to discuss in close and intimate detail with a total stranger.

Awesome.

When the door opened, I had myself in such a state of discombobulation I squeaked a little hello before even waiting to discover who it was had joined me. Instead of the handsome Dr. Mantegna, however, a woman's startled face had me clutching at the robe that more than sufficiently draped me in modesty.

"My apologies," she said with a flash of a smile, her slim and delicate build dressed in a pantsuit I instantly coveted—who didn't love a perfectly tailored pantsuit?—her dark hair pulled back from her pale face in a tight bun at the base of her neck, white button-up framing her heart-shaped face and flawless skin, green eyes expertly outlined in a thin application of black liner and mascara only showcasing her natural beauty. She held out one hand to me and I shook it despite the awkward situation. "Taylor Dulle, miss…?"

"Mrs.," I said. Almost blurted Fleming, caught myself. "Mandy Everett." I really needed to get ahold of myself.

"You're in excellent hands," she said. I really wished people would stop telling me that. It made me nervous, as if they felt they needed to appease me in some way. Shouldn't actions speak louder? Or maybe it was just my present state of mind making me cranky.

Yeah, you already know the answer to that, don't you?

"Are you a doctor?" I forced myself to relax somewhat as she shook her head, even as Che Mantegna stepped through, frowning at the sight of her.

"She is *not*," he said, crisp and short enough she flinched, though her smile remained, forced but present.

"Again, my apologies," she said. "I was looking for Dr. Mantegna and didn't know he was with a patient."

"Which I am," he said, gesturing at the door. "We can talk later, Taylor."

She instantly obeyed, waving a little to me on the way out, though the look she shot him wasn't as friendly as I expected. The moment she was gone, he turned to me with a genuine expression of regret and concern, sitting down across from me on his rolling stool.

"I'm so sorry about that," he said. "Ms. Dulle works for one of the drug companies that supplies the clinic. She knows better than to interrupt."

"It's all right," I said.

"No," he shook his head, grim now as he reached for a tablet on the counter. "It really isn't. It's an invasion of privacy, Mrs. Everett, and I'll make sure the clinic's management knows of her indiscretion. It will never happen again."

He must have been worried I'd sue or something. "As long as no one else wanders in," I said, letting out a nervous laugh.

Che's dark eyes sparkled, and he smiled back. "I certainly hope not," he said.

Just as the door opened and yet another interruption joined the fray.

This time, however, from his reaction, the woman who stopped in a hurry with a gasp and wide eyes as she spotted me had him sighing and shaking his head.

"I'm so sorry." She wore a suit of her own, A-line skirt falling a bit too far past her knees to carry off the look, her rounder body and slightly slumped posture doing nothing to carry the off-the-rack navy number. Yes, I was judging, down to her dumpy flats and the oversized pearl necklace she wore, but only because I was in a mood, you understand. Normally I wouldn't be so mean, even in my head. But she really needed to do something about the severe bleached bangs she wore over her squinting eyes and her lipstick's migration into the lines around her mouth? Gauche.

I seriously needed to take a breath.

"Phyllis," Che said.

"Phyllis Haines," she said, offering me her hand in a rush. I shook it, wondering what kind of place they were running around here when she went on. "Clinic administrator. You must be Mandy Everett." I nodded as she gushed on. "Your husband, Calvin, is a darling." Was he, now? I fought the twist of my lips at the descriptor, not because I didn't agree but because I was still lingering in the sting of our last conversation—correction, his chastisement—and wasn't sure I was willing to let it go or not.

"Was there something you needed, Phyllis?" Che's tone was warm enough, since this was his boss, after all. But there was a world-weariness to his patience that had me relaxing in his presence.

"Just a moment of your time, please." She bobbed her head to me. "If you'll excuse us?"

He looked like he was about to argue before he finally nodded, smiling at me as he stood. "I'll be right back." And left without further word, head down next to Phyllis as the pair whispered their way out of the room, closing the door behind them.

Now, there was no proof in the offing they were discussing anything to do with the case, but I let my intuition and natural nosiness guide me, slipping down off the table and heading for the exit. But when I poked my nose out into the quiet hall, it was empty. My gaze instead settled on a water dispenser perched in the far corner and, with the logical connection dehydration could make me grumpy poking my inner bear, I hurried to it and the paper cups provided, pouring myself a glass while feeling exposed and obvious despite being alone.

Something about being in a robe in public gave me a serious case of the heebies.

As I turned to head back to my exam room, I paused at the sound of voices through one of the doors, a man and woman's arguing tones stopping me in my tracks. But when I eased the door open to take a peek, it wasn't an exam room on the other side, but a corridor and, just past the threshold, I spotted not Che and Phyllis, as expected, but the short and angry Dr. Linder confronting a tall blonde woman with an earnest expression.

"You said we'd cleared up this misunderstanding, Ms. Sigler," Linder was saying. So, this was the FDA investigator Lloyd Aberstock was worried about?

"I said nothing of the sort," she shot back. Sounded to me like my friend had reason for concern. "New evidence has come to light that has me even more determined to ensure this trial isn't being influenced."

"Ridiculous," Linder snorted. "You're on a witch hunt, Ms. Sigler, and when your supervisor finds out you've been badgering me over unfounded rumors, I'll make sure it's your job on the line, not my trial."

"And when they find out you've been faking your data," she hissed in his face, "you'll be not only stripped of your medical license, Dr. Linder, you'll go to prison for malpractice and endangering patients by tampering with a drug trial."

Linder spluttered before pushing past her, stomping off while she watched him go, expression grim before she followed after him. I eased the door closed, scowling at my water glass, now furious myself at the arrogant doctor. If Lauren Sigler was right, Bernice was in danger, and I would not tolerate that.

Wow, I really *was* in a mood.

Trouble was, I had an exam to endure to keep my cover, though the last thing I wanted right now was to talk about myself or the looming pachyderm of possibility that had lurked in the back—and now forefront thanks to my realization—of my mind. I needed to work, to shake off this horrible feeling, the weight and pressure squeezing me into foul humor and a protective state of seething frustration I knew I'd end up taking out on someone who didn't deserve it while putting the case in jeopardy.

Which meant, naturally, I did the big girl panties thing. Jerked them firmly into place (metaphorically, at least), wrangled my inner redhead into semi-submission and headed back to the exam room to do my duty before I could change my mind and storm off to confront Linder in a thin robe and unreasonable rage.

I'd just settled, if you could call it that, sipping the water I'd almost forgotten in my distracted state when Dr. Che Mantegna returned. I have no idea what he saw on my face or in my posture, but instead of apologizing again, he instantly locked the door before crossing to me, sitting down and meeting my eyes with his own big, brown ones full of compassion.

"Tell me about your relationship with your husband," he said.

Why did that question make me burst into tears? Okay, I was already wound up, so maybe it was just a release I needed. Another one, the second for today. Better that I cried like that, however, than explode, right? Che kindly handed me a box of tissues, taking my water from me when I almost spilled it, letting me weep and blow my nose and vent out my emotional distress before he said another word.

"Better?" He handed back my water as I nodded and took a sip. "I know coming here was a huge decision," Che said, "and that there's a giant story behind you, and what likely feels like unsurmountable odds ahead. I know you are tired and wrung out and something that's supposed to be fun and easy and fulfilling has turned into a trial. A source of pain where there should be joy." He was talking about pregnancy, about having kids, I knew that intellectually. But his words spoke to my whole life, whether he knew it or not, and I found myself crying again, at least able to listen and absorb while the moisture tracked down my cheeks and the horrible tension around my heart broke and released. "I'm here for you, Mandy," he said. "For what's good for you and your body and, hopefully, your future children. I'm so sorry we were interrupted. And that you've had to endure what you've endured. But I'm on your side, no matter what and if you'll let me, we'll get through this together. Regardless of the outcome. Okay?"

"Has anyone told you you're a really great doctor?" I hiccupped and then laughed a little, sagging as the last of the emotional turmoil I'd been living under let go and washed clean, even my anger over Dr. Linder departing and leaving me wrung out but now capable of rational thought.

"A time or two," Che said. "Now, let's talk about your history."

Oh, he had no idea of the Pandora's box he just opened.

CHAPTER EIGHT

EXCEPT, OF COURSE, IT wasn't my actual history Dr. Che Mantegna was interested in, at least not the dead bodies I'd uncovered and the things I'd realized about myself after my return to Reading. My faint panic over having to discuss my cheating ex and my return home a decade after failing at life only to fall head-first into more trouble than I could actually recall ended abruptly when he asked his first question.

"When was the last time you and your husband were intimate?"

Um. Blush. Yikes. He meant *that* history.

Yup, he had much more personal questions to ask, and as I stammered and stuttered my way through the first few, Dr. Mantegna made a point of putting me at ease.

"It's just us here," he said, that kind smile returning. "I have your best interest at heart, I promise you that."

"Thank you, doctor," I said, covering my discomfort with an excuse. "I'm just not used to talking about this kind of thing to someone other than my best friend. Or Cr—Calvin."

"Please, call me Che," he said. "And I understand that. But if we're going to get to the bottom of why you're having trouble, I need you to be honest with me. I promise, no more interruptions and total discretion. Okay?"

I nodded and hoped Crew was going through this too because if I was the only one who had to answer embarrassing personal questions, I was going to punish both men who brought me here. For years.

Oddly, Che's whole kind routine did the job and while I still blushed a time or two, it was easier than I thought it would be to settle into frank discussion and even sparked my curiosity when he asked specific things I wasn't expecting. Che was happy to explain why he needed the answers he did and put me so at ease at last it was honestly easier to talk about my sex life than it would have been to reveal the inner me I originally thought he was going to expose.

That's not to say I wasn't annoyed with myself I couldn't be more professional about the whole thing. I was a grown woman and hardly unworldly. I guess I'd never been put into a position like this one before, with a specialist who was trying to help me (or thought he was). Usually, these kinds of conversations were much lewder and happened over margaritas with Daisy while we compared notes on men we'd dated.

So, it wasn't that I was a prude exactly, but he really was thorough. Rather than let the opportunity pass, however, I chose to settle into his professionalism and compassion and answer as completely as possible. By the end of our talk, I felt so comfortable with him that even though we'd barely met a few hours ago, I would have told him anything he wanted to know by the time he smiled and set aside his tablet.

He really was good at what he did. Which made me wonder why he'd given up this job to work under someone like Dr. Ian Linder. For the patients, perhaps? Whatever his reasons, I was grateful despite the fact this was supposed to be a cover story that I had Che to talk to and not someone like Bernice's physician.

"Thank you for being so honest," Che said. "If you're up for it, I'll call in the nurse and we'll finish up for today with your physical exam."

"Is Cr—Calvin going through this, too?" Way to almost blow his cover, Fee. Again. Yikes.

Che chuckled as he headed for the door, unlocking it and opening it, waving at someone on the other side. "Don't worry," the handsome doctor said as a smiling nurse entered, her silver hair a contrast to her youthful face. "He's not getting off easy either. But when we're done, we'll have the answers you need, so it's worth it."

A half-hour later, now vaguely hopeful and weary, truth be told, all the mental energy required to maintain my elevated emotional state expended and leaving me calm and accepting, I joined Crew in the small, interior garden bracketed by the glass walls of the clinic, open sky above bright blue but shielded from the outside world in a terrarium-like feel that maintained the hushed and protective illusion the inside created.

He looked up as I entered, his own expression rather bemused, warm hands holding mine as I sat next to him on the stone bench, his lips brushing my cheek and arm sliding around me when I leaned into him and sighed the deepest sigh I think I'd ever let out of me while I sagged into his strength.

"How did it go?" Crew's soft question had me pondering.

"I guess we'll see," I said, looking up into his blue eyes. "I've been thinking about it and didn't know it."

"Me too." He hesitated then. "Fee, are you worried?"

"I think I was," I said. "Funny, right? We're not here for this, but it's a thing, Crew."

He nodded then, lips pressing to my forehead. "No matter what," he whispered, "I love you, Fiona Fleming. You know that, right?"

I hugged him then, snuggling my nose into the hollow of his neck just above his collarbone, my favorite because I fit there so perfectly, his scent filling my senses, his warmth heating me up. "I love you, too," I said, not surprised this time that tears surfaced, and even welcoming them since the desperate pressure of my previous emotional state had vanished. This felt more natural, without the overwhelm I'd been fighting, so I let them rise, only to have the feeling dissipate without needing to cry. Huh, so that was how this worked. "No matter what."

He held me a long time, the silence rather nice, and though I knew we were there for a different reason, having those stolen moments with him meant more to me than anything. For the first time in a long time, I felt truly connected to the man I loved. Like my concerns about children, I had no idea I'd been feeling this level of disconnect, though if I looked back and was honest with myself, the distance had less to do with his work habits and more with my choice to judge him for doing what he loved while assuming that meant he put me second.

When in fact? He was putting us first in the best way he knew how.

Our lovely interlude could only last so long, of course, but logically knowing that and living it were two different things. That's why my irritation at being interrupted caught me off guard when two people stormed into the oasis of greenery only to stop about ten feet away to have their little tiff inside my circle of love and joy.

Damn it.

Crew tensed next to me, the pair just visible past the towering plant that shaded our bench, the sight of Dr. Ian Linder making me scowl, though the woman who confronted him was equally annoying in her strident and elevated tone.

"Talk to me!" She stood in his way, one hand on his arm, her head wrapped in a lovely green scarf of her own, making me guess she was one of his trial patients. "Ian, please, I just want you to talk to me."

"I already told you," he said, gruff and cold, "your test results—"

"I don't care about the stupid trial!" She practically wailed that at him while he flinched, distaste on his face, body pulling away from her as she tried to get closer to him. "I care about us, our marriage. Don't you see that? Can't you see *me*?" She finally backed away when he crossed his arms over his chest, his expression settling into chilly denial. "You don't," she said then, barely above normal speaking volume, heartbreaking to me as she shifted from demanding and pleading to acceptance. "You never did. I'm a disease to you. And that's all I'll ever be."

He didn't say anything, hands dropping to his sides when her head bowed, his face twisting through a variety of emotions that had me wanting to shake him. Instead of comforting the woman who claimed to be his wife, Dr. Ian Linder instead stiffened at last, nodding.

"Your recovery is remarkable," he said. "Like the rest of the patients in the trial. You should be grateful, Sandra." With that, he pushed past her and exited the garden, leaving the woman to cup her face in her hands and cry.

That man was truly an ass and a half.

She finally turned to leave herself, only then realizing she wasn't alone. With a low cry, Sandra Linder ran from the garden, weeping and visibly embarrassed, while my husband hugged me tightly. When I looked up, I noted the tightness of his jaw, the anger dominating his expression, meeting his eyes when he met my gaze with another sigh.

"If I'm ever that big of a jerk," he said.

"Impossible," I said. And filled him in on what I'd overheard.

Back to work then, Fiona Fleming.

It didn't take long to return to focus mode, something that actually felt better now that I'd cleansed myself of the weight of emotion I'd been carrying. Which meant I no longer read anything into our partnership, or that it was Crew who reached out to Kit to look into Ian Linder. Neither did he seem put out that I contacted Liz, his former partner, about Lauren Sigler. Instead, as the next half hour passed and we did what we did best, it felt far more like he and I were finally in sync than treading on one another's toes.

I know I use the word *awesome* frequently with much sarcasm attached but. Yeah. Awesome.

By the time we'd done what we could, I was ready to take on the world. And dinner with the Aberstocks.

CHAPTER NINE

I HAD BEEN HOPING for a quiet meal with our friends, a chance to catch up without having to worry about accidentally revealing our true identities along the way. That plan came to a crashing halt when we arrived in the dining room an hour later to discover Bernice and Lloyd—more than likely the former than the latter—had invited another patient to join us. Imagine our surprise when none other than Sandra Linder looked up from her conversation with the lovely Mrs. Aberstock, her vague horror transmuting into shame and guilt as she quickly glanced away again, cheeks pink with the flush of embarrassment.

With nothing to be done about it but a quick coverup, I smiled my best welcoming expression,

Crew sitting beside Lloyd, while I firmly introduced myself and my husband to the anxious woman.

"Bernice says the loveliest things about you," Sandra said, her nervousness fading somewhat when neither of us brought up our first and most unfortunate encounter.

"She says the loveliest things about everyone," I laughed, watching Sandra Linder relax even more while I threw Bernice a fond smile, too. "Isn't she just the sweetest?"

Sandra nodded instantly, hand reaching out to squeeze my friend's. "She really is. I don't know what I would have done without her the last few weeks."

"Now, you two," Bernice said, blushing herself. "Aren't you just darlings for saying so? You'll give this old lady a big head."

"Well-deserved, my dear," Lloyd spoke up, adoring gaze locked on the love of his life.

"Stop, all of you," Bernice said with a breathless laugh. "I wonder what's for dinner? Mandy, you'll love the chef here." Bless her for using my made-up identity. "He's almost as good as your mother."

"Your mother is a chef?" Sandra perked at that, now completely at ease with me while Crew chatted with Lloyd under his breath, likely filling my Dr. Aberstock in on what we'd uncovered (not much, true, but an update no less).

"She's an amazing cook," I said, thinking about Mom and her incredible talents. "And a baker like no other."

"Lucy is just brilliant," Bernice gushed. "Her

chocolate cake will put you in raptures."

"Sounds divine," Sandra said. "It feels like forever since I had sugar." Her expression shifted into discontent.

"Why is that?" I looked back and forth between both women while they shared an eye roll of mutual unhappiness.

"Sugar feeds the disease, dear," Bernice said. "At least, according to all the current research."

"No cake," Sandra said in audible despair, though clearly accentuated with amusement as well. "No ice cream." They both groaned. "And forget about brownies, cookies, even pudding."

"I hate pudding," Bernice said to me, "but I'd kill you for a cup of chocolate right now." They giggled together, the sadness of it mitigated by their willing acceptance and the way they embraced their fates. I understood the need to tap into humor to soften the truths they lived every day thanks to cancer, but it still hurt my heart knowing they not only had to suffer the horrible reality of the disease, it stripped away anything that could bring even an ounce of joy just to keep them going in the hope of finding a cure.

Made me even more furious Dr. Linder might be a fraud.

The first course was a lovely carrot soup I actually adored, though the lack of salt had me squirming and wishing I'd snuck in a shaker from home. By the time the second course—a light salad with olive oil and balsamic barely gracing the greens—was done, my stomach was begging for real food. As a distraction—and means to get this job wrapped up so I could save Bernice and go home to my mother's cooking I now craved—I excused myself to go to the washroom without the intent to follow through.

Not that I purposely abandoned my table mates to snoop, but. Okay, I did. Tell me you're not surprised? Dinnertime could prove to be useful, after all, and I found myself in the midst of self-congratulation when I noted the distinct lack of staff lingering anywhere near the dining room while the patients enjoyed their meals. Which meant my real goal, a look in Dr. Linder's office, might actually be attainable. Worth a shot, at least, if only to keep me from longing for something more substantial to fill my stomach.

If they tried to make me vegan in this place? They had another thing coming because you better believe Crew would be driving to the nearest fast-food joint for a burger if I didn't get a hit of meat before bed.

I didn't make it nearly as far as my initial arrogance suggested I could. I'd rightly guessed the doorway behind the front desk led to the offices, and made it down the first hallway without incident, but was forced to stop and wait around a corner near the entry to the main office at the sound of voices arguing. And though I recognized both, I was surprised to find not only was Dr. Linder unpopular with staff, at odds with the FDA and mean to patients, it seemed even the facility administrator had her issues dealing with the man. At least, that was the gist I got from the fury in Phyllis Haines's voice as she snapped at the researcher just as I settled in to eavesdrop.

"And I told you," she snarled, "I'm done dealing with the FDA, Ian. If you can't get a handle on this—"

"Don't threaten me, Phyllis," he growled back. "You know full well your little clinic only got funding for the fertility project because I'm here running my cancer research. What do you think would happen if I took my trial elsewhere?"

She sucked in a loud breath. I didn't dare peek around the corner, just in case, knowing I was on the verge of getting caught but needing to hear her response. "How dare you," she said. "This is ridiculous."

"Is it?" Ian's voice dropped in volume but not in vitriol. "Stay out of my way, Phyllis. You don't want to cross me." The sound of feet stomping away was followed by a huffing sound that was clearly from the administrator.

I almost turned and headed back right then and there. The offices were just past this corner and there was no way I'd be gaining access without getting caught. At least, not without a good reason for being back here or the cover of darkness. But just before I spun to hurry away, someone else spoke, a woman's voice addressing Phyllis, a voice I recognized.

"I'm sorry to bother you, Ms. Haines," Norma, the front desk receptionist, said, "but Mrs. Marshall is asking about her necklace again."

"Darn it," Phyllis tsked. "It hasn't turned up?"

"Not yet," Norma said, sounding concerned. "That's the fourth personal item this month. What do you want me to do?"

Well now. Not that it had anything to do with Bernice's case, but it sounded to me like Phyllis Haines had a theft problem on her hands.

"I'll deal with it," she said with such abruptness my eyebrows shot up. "Thank you, Norma. That will be all."

I almost missed the sound of feet approaching and barely had time to turn and sprint back to the main lobby before I was spotted, pausing near the desk to catch my breath as Norma emerged from the back with a frown on her face. The moment she spotted me, she smiled, nodding.

"I'm lost," I said, forcing a smile. "The washroom?"

She quickly guided me back into the hallway leading to the dining room before hurrying off herself. Which left me to return to our table where a vegetable casserole waited for me. I knew it. No meat.

I really needed to solve this case quickly.

My discontent with dinner, tied to the lack of progress I'd made in my vain attempt to poke my nose in where it wasn't wanted, had me squirming all over again. By the time we said goodbye to the Aberstocks and Sandra Linder, Crew practically dragged me to our room where he faced me down with some heat.

"We're trying not to draw attention to ourselves,"

he said.

"Excuse me," I snapped back, emotional state clearly not as recovered as I thought. "While that's true, I'm also trying to do my job here." I hated I sounded petulant, but it came out that way.

"Where did you run off to?" Like he had to ask, accusation already in his eyes.

"I already told you," I said. "To do my job."

Crew heaved a frustrated sigh, slipping the glasses from his face, that raised vein in his temple and the corded ligaments in his neck sure signs of his temper rising. "We're in this together," he said.

He was right, of course, he was right. "I tried to get into the main office," I said, not as graciously as I could have, but answering him, so there was that, right?

His exasperation had me tightening up all over again, stomach clenched against his judgment. "In the middle of dinner," he said, words dripping sarcasm, "without a story. And no," he cut me off before I could speak up past the inhale of sharp breath I took, "I know you, Fiona Fleming. You didn't have a cover story. Did you?"

He didn't need to glare at me like that, all self-righteous and such. "I saw an opportunity and I took it," I said.

"You put our case at risk," Crew told me, slow and careful, "because you're impatient."

"I've solved more than enough crimes in the past I think my track record speaks for my technique." Oh, huffy now, was I? You betcha. Mostly because I knew he was right, and I was being an idiot.

Crew let out a long, ragged breath before speaking again. "I realize we have two very different sets of skills," he said, really being far kinder than I deserved and while I knew it intellectually, I couldn't manage to bring myself back from the emotional edge I found myself on again, "and opposite styles, but I need you to please, Fee, just please think things through before you act from now on. Okay?"

I offered a stiff nod. "You know, I've managed just fine all along." Why did I throw that at him like a weapon?

"And how many times have you put yourself in danger, to the point you've almost been hurt or killed?" He shot that back, his salvo much more effective than mine. Which only made me angrier, not diffused.

"I guess we do it your way then," I said, turning my back on him, sitting abruptly on the couch with my arms and legs crossed, logic yelling at me to stop this ridiculous behavior while my stupid ego snarked and slunk its way into resentment.

Crew stood there a long moment, silent and still, before turning and retreating to the bathroom, closing the door behind him. He didn't slam it or anything, but he didn't have to.

Fine, be like that.

Oh, Fee.

CHAPTER TEN

CREW DID EXIT EVENTUALLY, face schooled to stiff calm, taking a seat on the bed with his phone while I angrily paged through a book on mine I didn't read a word of.

After what seemed like forever—but was simply a long, silent and uncomfortable four hours—Crew finally stood, darkness outside the windows stretching his shadow as the one lonely light he turned on not so long ago cast his tall body against the door.

"It's just midnight," he said like I couldn't even be trusted to read the time. "If we're going to have a shot at sneaking into Linder's office, it's now."

I followed his lead without a word, so I take credit for that much, even as I stewed inwardly over what was wrong with me. My husband was completely right. I'd done a stupid thing sneaking off without him, taking a dumb chance of getting caught when it was Bernice's health and well-being in the balance. But something about the way this was unfolding had me on edge and I had to admit it to myself as we both paused at the foyer, it had nothing to do with Crew, not really. And everything to do with the fact I'd been on my own from day one without support from him or Dad—not really—and now all of a sudden, when it really mattered, I was relegated to second chair.

My ego was a total jerkface. And, on alert, it turned out, because I was the one to spot Dr. Ian Linder heading at a stomping pace toward the front doors, coming into the clinic's foyer from outside despite the late hour, forcing us to hide behind a rather impressive greenery collection consisting of ferns and bamboo while the researcher stormed his way toward the offices and disappeared.

"Crap," Crew said.

Tell me about it. "Let's look for a back door." Why hadn't that thought occurred to me before? He flashed me a grin and a nod, the pair of us retreating back the way we'd come, that choice reinforced when a tall man in a dark uniform appeared from the entry to another wing and seated himself behind the reception desk. We managed to evade his notice, but it was clear to me now there was no way into the office area without security seeing us.

Back door it was.

It didn't take much to exit through a side door onto the manicured pathway that led around the building, the lack of security surprising but serving us, at least. By the time we'd crept around to the rear of the building cluster, I was starting to doubt this course of action. But, as we cleared the last corner and peeked into the staff parking lot on the far side, it was easy enough to not only spot the security cameras but to avoid them.

Crew shook his head with visible disgust at the lack of adequate surveillance, and I had to agree with him. Sure, the fact there wasn't a live guard back here, too, made our job easier, the obvious cost-cutting measure didn't bode well for the Your Best Life Clinic, did it? Such an expensive and well-appointed facility shirking on security couldn't be a good sign.

Time to look into Phyllis Haines and this place too, apparently.

It was also obvious to me the administrator was more worried about her employees than she was the safety of her patients since the only security camera at the back door was aimed at the parking lot and the staff's cars there. I made mental note again of the conversation I'd overheard and wondered if the theft problem went beyond the loss of personal items and might be endemic of the entire facility. With this laxity in the watchfulness of the actual clinic and attention to what might be leaving it instead of coming in, I found myself drawing conclusions that had me even more concerned for Bernice's health and well-being.

Not that I was complaining about our ease of entry, mind you. Even if there was no cause for worry ultimately and Lloyd Aberstock's fears appeased by our investigation, Phyllis Haines would be receiving a detailed report from Fleming Investigations about her either utter disregard or idiocy when it came to the security of her clinic.

Without a soul in sight, Crew opened the door for me, the pair of us sneaking inside the dark hallway, the administration office easy to find thanks to blatant signage. And though I kept alert and didn't let the lax security make me less vigilant, the pair of us managed to comb through not only Phyllis's office, but that of her assistant as well without finding anything of note.

"Let's check on Linder," Crew whispered as we exited the main office. "I figured this would be a waste of time, but we had it to spend."

I agreed. "Hopefully he's gone by now." I followed my husband, letting him take the lead, the earlier resurgence of my resentment gone in the focus of the investigation. Sure, we were kind of breaking the law, but if Linder was as well—and if Phyllis Haines was putting patients at risk—we were both willing to at least poke around as long as we didn't unlock any doors. That meant garbage cans and open offices were fair game. Yeah, sophistry, I get it. Our presence under fake names meant we were walking a very thin legal line and anything we found could be thrown out of court if it came to that.

But since we weren't building a case against Dr. Linder per se, only providing information for Lloyd and Bernice, even my former FBI husband didn't seem to have qualms about toeing this particular line.

Mind you, getting caught in Rhode Island with out-of-state licenses? Could have pretty dodgy repercussions. Which meant we shouldn't get caught, right? More reason for me to listen to my husband and the warning he tried to deliver. Why then did I still bristle against being handled?

We stopped at the central area of the administration offices, in what looked like a crossing of corridors. I recognized the hallway across from us as the one I'd hidden in earlier in the evening during dinner, so we were definitely in the right area. But before either of us could make a move to check and see if Linder was in his office, the sound of footfalls—heavy ones not trying to hide, meaning someone who was supposed to be here was coming—drove us both back and through a door into what amounted to a broom closet.

Always with the storage rooms, seriously.

It was dark enough that I was comfortable peeking out over my husband's shoulder as he snuck a look through the crack he left open, the sight of Phyllis Haines hurrying by with a worried and almost angry look on her face making me wonder what drew her back after hours as well. Could it have to do with Linder? Seemed oddly coincidental the pair of them were here well after midnight. We stayed put, Crew nodding to me and then toward the crack where I took another look, wondering why Brooke Poplar snuck past our hideaway, her own expression tight and anxious. She was heading in the same direction as Phyllis, deeper into the offices, forcing us to wait and stay quiet while I could only hope they'd leave so we could dig around for what we came here to find—or not.

Turned out this part of the building was far more active late at night than we'd expected, the weird appearance of Taylor Dulle walking quickly with her head down making me frown as she strode past. What was the drug rep doing back here so late? Followed almost on her heels by Che Mantegna, huh. And then, at a quick but quiet pace, Lauren Sigler bringing up the rear.

The final visitor at least had reason to be here as far as I was concerned, though Sandra Linder's equally skulking entry seemed much more in line with Crew and me than someone with a legitimate reason for visiting her own husband.

Crew turned to me, easing the door closed all the way, bending to press his lips to my ear. "Something's not right."

Tell me about it. "Should we try again tomorrow?"

He shook his head, though it took him a long moment before he did so, and only after the sound of footsteps retreating had us both holding still and quiet again. When he peeked one last time, we both observed the odd exodus of everyone we'd seen enter, though in reverse, Sandra fleeing, Lauren hoofing it, barely out of sight of Che and Taylor who spoke with their heads together, whispering as they passed us. Brooke didn't reappear, likely returned to the main building via the other corridor, but Phyllis did and, I had to say, as she almost ran past us, the terror on her face when she turned to look back over her shoulder had my stomach clenching.

What was going on?

We waited another five minutes that felt like hours before Crew eased the door open, my impatience barely contained as my much more careful husband cocked his head, clearly listening for oncoming footsteps. He let me pass, closing the door behind us with a near-silent click, easing forward and around the corner, heading to the right, the same direction the people we'd observed had come from.

It wasn't hard to locate Dr. Linder's office door, his name on a plate screwed to the wall next to it. I let Crew try the handle, felt relief wash over me as it turned easily, and followed him inside, catching my breath in my lungs until we were safely within, and the door closed behind us. Only then did I exhale in a slow and careful release, Crew flashing me a grin in the dim light coming through the tall window behind Linder's desk.

"Let's be quick," my husband said. "You try the desk. I'll take the filing cabinet." He was already on the move, and I didn't waste time either, hurrying to the rear of the room and grasping the back of the office chair, turning it toward me with a plan to sit down in it.

Tripped over something on the floor, looked down at the black cable and box lying on the carpet, the loose laptop plug dangling over the arm of the chair and to the floor.

Oh, but that wasn't all, was it? No, because my intent to take a load off? Wasn't going to go the way I planned. Trouble was, the seat was already occupied. And while I might have had a real problem on my hands if Dr. Ian Linder was capable of noticing my obvious trespassing, he was already well past being able to complain to anyone about our presence.

Another dead body. This was becoming a habit I could live without (no pun intended).

CHAPTER ELEVEN

I PACED MY ROOM, unable to slow down my brain or my excessively beating heart despite the fact this was hardly the first corpse I'd stumbled over. It was, however, the first time I hadn't immediately made a call to the authorities to alert them to the presence of said deceased person. Instead, with Crew's grim expression making me even more anxious, my husband rapidly herded me toward the office door where he did a hasty wipe-down of the handle after rushing back to the chair to rub away my fingerprints from the leather surface.

I didn't argue with him, the two of us making a miraculous return to the room assigned us clear of any interference or encounters despite how busy this place seemed to have been at the least opportune moments. So apparently uncovering evidence to help friends was met with universal resistance while reporting a dead body?

Not so much.

Good to know, thanks for that.

Crew, for his part, seemed qualm-free, making quiet calls as I unfolded my pacing routine with the aggressive stomping gait of a soldier marching into a battle she knew she was going to lose. How my husband kept his perspective and cool I could only attribute to his FBI training, because I was on the verge of losing my mind over the fact a dead man now sat, undiscovered and abandoned, in a leather office chair one annex away from where I fought my conscience and the need to panic-dial state police to come and cart his sad and sorry carcass to the morgue for immediate autopsy.

Oh, were you perhaps running on the assumption that Dr. Ian Linder's death might have been accidental or perhaps even self-inflicted? Natural causes, maybe? Yeah, like I'd be that lucky. You better believe I took the time needed to do my own brief and, sadly, familiar investigation of the corpse—no touching, mind you, but contact wasn't necessary—before Crew and I booked it out of the dead man's office and landed back here. That's how I knew beyond a shadow of a doubt the doctor in question had been murdered.

You need proof? I present exhibits A through C for your perusal. Ahem. Beginning with, but not exclusive to, A) the petechia of his eyes where hemorrhage had left behind tell-tale marks of loss of oxygen. Alone, perhaps, not sufficient evidence, until paired with B) the red line of a narrow implement used to cut off the air supply clearly demarked on his throat just below the jawline. And, if that still leaves lingering doubt, I present Exhibit C) the protruding pale blue pill signaling the presence of more than one, it turned out, hanging from his bulging tongue.

I'd already bagged the one pill I'd liberated from his open mouth, the rather sizable medication tablet in its oblong glory tucked carefully inside a zippered plastic bag and now lying in indiscreet accusation at the foot of the bed. The fact I carried unused zipper bags in my luggage might come as a surprise to you, but should it, really? Considering my track record? The tissue I'd nabbed from the box on Linder's desk to carry the tell-tale pill back to our room had accompanied the evidence into said bag, not that its presence made me feel any better.

I took a vital clue from a crime scene and hadn't told the cops about it.

What was I thinking?

Crew hung up on his most recent call, joining me as I paced, one hand on my elbow finally stopping my endless circling of the room, meeting my eyes with his own calm and filled with comforting confidence. "Let's sit," he said. "Fee, it's going to be okay."

I jabbed a finger at the pill on the bed, the shining plastic accusing me of wrongdoing. "It's *not*," I said, voice shaking, stomach doing a slow roll.

"It is." He hugged me and though I longed to sag into him and trust him, I couldn't bring myself to relax from the rigid tension gripping me in a fist of iron. "Sweetheart, we couldn't break our cover. Especially now."

"Why?" I shoved gently against him, but with firm intent, Crew releasing me and not looking happy about it. "We need to call the police, Crew. Tell them what we know."

"Which is what?" He tossed his hands before tucking them both into his front pockets, frown turning to calm again. "Babe, we don't know anything. Linder is dead, yes." He acknowledged my panicked splutter before I could utter it. "But we don't know who killed him or why."

I pointed at the pill again in utter silence.

"Exactly," Crew said then. "For all we know, this is tied to the trial. If it is, that means Bernice is in real danger. And we're here for her, right?" I managed a nod. Where had this irrational panic come from? Crew was right, and yet I couldn't bring myself to adopt his casual and composed posture even for a moment. "Not to mention we found him when we were trespassing. Fee." My husband caught my shoulders in his big hands, blue eyes intent and insistent. "We won't be able to help anyone if we're arrested or kicked out because we were somewhere we weren't legally supposed to be."

He was totally and utterly correct. Without a doubt, down to the ground, completely accurate and logical. So why did I feel so wretchedly guilty?

"Linder will be found soon enough," my husband said, turning away to begin his own pacing, though his seemed methodical and far too controlled to compare to my frantic spins around the room. Definitely FBI training. So unfair. "I'm more worried Lloyd might be right than I am about leaving the good doctor to be found by others."

Okay, that was fair. "What did Dad say?" Because of course, Crew called Dad, right?

"He agreed," Crew said. Of course, he did. The stoic duo had me flanked. "And so did Liz." Awesome, though Elizabeth Michaud was former Bureau too, so she didn't count. "He's going to call back in a minute. A group talk is in order." Speak of the devil and he'll dial your number because Crew's phone chose that moment to ring.

I forced myself to sit on the sofa, my husband perched next to me, as he answered. "John."

"Crew," Dad's deep and graveled voice answered.

"Gang," Liz said in her own cool and crisp alto.

"Are you okay, Fee?" That from Jill Wagner. The former sheriff of Reading and now Fleming Investigations PI at our Montpelier office with Liz was the only one I might be able to count on to have my back.

"We need to contact the authorities," I blurted.

"Fee," Dad said, tone reasonable and as patient as Crew's had been, "that's a terrible idea."

"Agreed," Liz clipped. "You call the state police now and you'll be either in cuffs or out of there so fast you won't be able to help anyone."

"Fee, I have to side with them," Jill said, apology in her voice. "The last thing you want is to lose your license, you or Crew. You're there as a favor to Dr. Aberstock, I know. But you technically broke the law in another state where you're not registered as a PI." I hadn't thought of that. "I wanted to protest this idea from the get-go, but it's Lloyd and Bernice." I could see the worry on Jill's face without being in her presence, coming through loud and clear in her tone. So much for having my back. She had even more logical reasons lined up to keep me from doing what felt like the only honest thing I could. Which only made it worse I knew I had to listen. "Please, I know this feels wrong, but it's for the best for everyone."

With my only chance at backup abandoning me to truth and clarity of thought, I finally exhaled, trying to ease that knot of wretchedness inside my stomach clenching itself around the base of my spine and giving me a horrible case of heartburn. "Fine," I said, glaring at the carpet under my feet, not meaning the word even a little bit and positive everyone else knew it, too. Because nothing about this was fine, was it? "We keep our mouths shut and out of the way. But then what?"

"We need to stay focused on why we're actually here," Crew said. Why did that ping my last nerve? Make fury bubble in my stomach against him when he didn't actually mean I wasn't keeping the Aberstocks in perspective over the dead man. Right?

Uh-huh. Sure sounded like it.

"It seems to me Lloyd had good reason to

worry," Dad said. "It's all hands on deck until we get this sorted, agreed?"

I grunted in response when everyone else managed a chipper word of acknowledgment. Which meant I barely heard a word as Dad quickly and efficiently handed out assignments. It wasn't until he said my name that I snapped partially out of my seething anger and unsettled mind.

"Fee." I glared at the phone like he could see me. "You and Crew need to keep your heads down and be our eyes and ears at the clinic. But don't take any chances. We're hitting the research on our end. Until we have something solid and actionable, you two are just patients like everyone else. Okay?"

I didn't answer, the rest of them signing off until it was just me and Crew and his dark phone.

"Bed," my husband said, leaning in to kiss my cheek. "You need rest, Fee."

I stood abruptly, nodding, hugging myself. "If you say so," I snapped. And locked myself in the bathroom.

Can you tell I just loved being bullied into doing what other people wanted when I knew better?

I did finally go to bed, turning away from my husband who made a brief effort to hold my hand. His heavy sigh didn't help, guilt over how I was treating him when he really was on our side only adding to my internal discomfort. It was a restless sleep, my tossing and turning and mind spinning meaning by the time I crawled out of bed shortly after dawn, I was in no better a mood than I had been when I'd laid down.

Crew kept his mouth shut, quiet and withdrawn, the two of us moving around one another as we prepared for breakfast in an uncomfortable silence that had me near to tears when I let myself think about it. I was on the verge of apologizing, my heart heavy and still not sure why I was letting this situation get to me over someone like Dr. Ian Linder. Especially when the sound of running feet and shouting had the two of us looking up and meeting one another's eyes like nothing else could.

Moments later, I hung back with Crew as the crowd of staff and patients watched two EMTs wheel a body bag on a gurney out through the lobby and into the morning sunshine while a distraught Phyllis Haines wept in the company of a rumpled looking suit.

I knew the look, didn't need the pair of uniforms he brought with him to identify the man speaking with Phyllis. Homicide detective, had to be. Finally. But effective and engaged or going through the motions? His abilities remained to be seen.

Not judging or anything.

CHAPTER TWELVE

CREW HELD BACK WHILE I slowly circled closer to the administrator and the suit she spoke to, noting the two uniforms who held the gathering back with just their presence. The rumpled detective reminded me of Rowan Mallory enough I didn't disregard him, knowing brilliant minds could easily hide behind façades of slovenliness, though the man's unkempt, graying hair and lack of enthusiasm as he spoke to Phyllis had me wondering.

Then again, if I had to deal with the weeping and horrified administrator, I might have been standoffish too. That was one benefit of not being in the thick of things, I suppose, though I was hard-pressed to feel anything but irritated about my lack of access to the unfolding drama.

Yeah, maybe I'd been in the middle of things too many times and for far too long to just step aside and let others take over. Ego or arrogance or both, did it matter? The truth was I was on the outside looking in and wasn't so high and mighty myself I understood my internal quandary.

I'd been severed from the excitement, and I was not happy about it. What did that say about me, then?

Dr. Che Mantegna pushed past one of the uniforms to join Phyllis, his warm face pale and ashen, hands trembling as he gently supported the woman, visibly shaken by what he'd just heard.

Or had he? Crew and I had both seen him just a few hours ago sneaking around the back offices near Dr. Linder's place of death. Che could have been a good actor, right? So could Phyllis, for that matter, along with the shortlist of other suspects I now considered, as each of them made an appearance.

Brooke Parlor stood off to one side with her arm around Sandra Linder, her frown more angry than sad, though the widow seemed suitably brokenhearted despite her husband's lack of emotional connection to her. As for the drug rep, Taylor Dulle, she seemed interested but not overly worked up at the news of Ian Linder's passing, so either she wasn't connected to his murder at all, or she was a sociopath who had no problem killing someone and getting away with it.

Fee Fleming. Judgy this morning, what?

When it came to Lauren Sigler, however, the FDA investigator looked to me like she'd been punched in the gut, as shocked as Che appeared to be, if not actively weeping like Sandra and Phyllis.

I didn't get to speak to anyone directly, the administrator pulling herself together as the detective backed away, gesturing at the two officers who immediately cut off any entry to the office wing.

"I'm so sorry," Phyllis said to the gathering, her voice shaking and cracking while she warbled her way through her duty. "There's been a terrible accident." Huh, not from what I'd seen, but okay, if she wanted to play it that way. "Please, if you could all go back to the dining room, Detective Prouse and his team have work to do here. Norma, Henry." She snapped her fingers in their direction, the head of reception and the orderly who I'd met yesterday instantly joining her. "Take care of our patients, please. I have to finish with these officers."

And that, it seemed, was that. With reinforcement built around the reason I disagreed with not revealing the dead body to the authorities, we might have remained with our cover intact, but my temper now simmered in steady irritation at being cut out of the investigation thanks to circumstances beyond my control. Oh, and only made worse when I found myself sitting in a bit of a huff at the breakfast table while a nervous young woman delivered stone-cut oatmeal, fruit and almond milk.

Seriously. Were they trying to set me off on purpose?

Okay, I wasn't unaware of my spike in emotional angst and did my best as I caught my own attention with the stabbing aggressiveness my spoon made at the nutty cereal offering sufficiently to force a deep breath and manage a smile for Bernice Aberstock as she settled next to me, eyes wide and face pale.

"You heard," she whispered, one hand settling on mine. I instantly put aside my own issues and held her fingers gently, nodding because nothing could calm me down like worrying about her.

"Bernice," I said, fully intending to tell her and Lloyd everything in my next few words.

"It's terrible," Crew cut me off, leaning into both Aberstocks across my body, shutting me down as he shook his head with a frown. "I'm so sorry, Bernice. I hope this doesn't interfere with your trial."

Lloyd looked back and forth between us, Crew's steady gaze surely at odds with my lip twitching and heated cheeks. He was a smart man. He had to know something was amiss. But as my husband met my eyes, his own hand sliding under the tablecloth to squeeze my knee, I got the message loud and clear.

Shut it, Fee.

I did. But not for the reason he wanted. Oh, no. Because if I did open my mouth at that moment? It would be to tell him where to go, how to get there, what to do when he arrived and that if he ever came back and treated me like that again? His would be the next corpse found.

Correction. His body would *never* be found.

Snarl.

I made it through breakfast. Miracles happen, right? I may have muttered the occasional word under my breath and did very little in the way of actually communicating with anyone during that meal, but I made it. And Crew wasn't dead yet. Yet being the operative word. In fact, I even managed a hug and a smile of sympathy for Bernice, a silent glare for Lloyd (willing him to read my mind and save my husband from certain death) and (be proud) made the journey all the way back to my room without losing my crap.

Once the door closed on me, though? All bets were off.

Except Crew beat me to it, shutting me down before I could shout a word. Because shouting was going to happen if he liked it or not.

"I know," he said. Stopped and let me digest that bit of information. "You're right, Fee. I feel terrible lying to them." He did, did he? The wave of heat that raced through me, overwhelming me thanks to my present inability to let it escape, meant the roaring sound in my head was a warning the steam pressure valve that was my temper was about to either explode for lack of outlet or give me an aneurism. But he was being reasonable, and I needed to be too, didn't I? Act the grownup? "We don't know anything more than they do at this point," Crew went on. "Why upset Bernice further until we have something concrete to say? Dr. Ian Linder is dead. His death may or may not have anything to do with the trial. And the trial is why we're here."

"The trial," I said, shocked at the detached tone of voice that emerged from me, not a hint of my temper in the icy coolness of it, "is over, Crew. No Dr. Linder, no drug trial." I caught my breath before my tone rose a few decibels. "They deserve to know about the accusation Lauren Sigler made. And that I found drugs in the dead man's mouth." I jabbed at my suitcase, the evidence now safely tucked away in my belongings. "Drugs that are more than likely the same ones he was using in the trial."

"We don't know that." Crew was finally heating up, too, it seemed, that vein popping up on his forehead, the under-eye tic I hadn't seen in a long time making an appearance. It was a regular feature when we'd first butted heads. I guess working together wasn't the great idea I'd thought it was. "This is what you do," he said then, tossing his hands, turning away from me. "You jump to conclusions and blurt out things you should keep to yourself and make a big mess." He stopped then, spun on me, regret crossing his face.

Far too late for that, my love. "I see," I said, now chilled to the bone and my temper gone so far past the heat of the moment it turned to freezing fury in a heartbeat. I felt as though a glacier had taken its place but welcomed it since cold was far more manageable than fire. And, in this case, dangerous. "Nice to finally hear what you really think, Crew. How grand of you to deign to share your thoughts about my investigative skills." I was on a roll, believe it, and it was going to take a miracle to slow down the racing freight train he'd set in motion. "And yet, it's been this mess I make that's solved, what? Twenty murders? Wait, more?" He flinched, jaw jumping. "Still, you're right. I'm hasty and unprofessional and clearly, I'm terrible at what I do so I'm just going to sit right here," I planted myself on the sofa, "and let my big, strong, smart husband take care of things since I'm obviously in the way and wrong."

"Fee." Crew didn't even bother to try to say more than my name. And didn't have time, because in that long and painful silence between us, someone knocked on the door.

"Time for your next tests," Brooke Poplar said as she entered a moment later, smile fading at the sight of both of us. Sure, I should probably have done my best to pretend not to be furious, but it wasn't like couples who came for this kind of testing didn't have their moments. Let's call it performance authenticity and leave it at that, shall we?

I stood and crossed to the door, not bothering to look back, reining myself in and doing what I was told because this was for Bernice.

As for Crew Turner, he was on his own.

CHAPTER THIRTEEN

IT WORKED OUT FOR the best. The last thing I wanted was to have any kind of conversation with my husband at the moment, knowing it wouldn't be productive and likely hurtful on both sides. That's why when we were separated again for our next round of testing I took it as an omen I was meant to stew on my own and sort my head and heart out before I made an even bigger mess out of a disaster from an overreact. I was surprised, however, when an attractive woman in her mid-forties entered my room this time, stethoscope around her neck and tablet in her hand suggesting she wasn't another accidental arrival.

"Where's Dr. Mantegna?" Did that come out complaining and aggressive? Probably, and though she was a newcomer and I normally would have done my best to be friendly, I just didn't have it in me at the moment. I felt myself tense as the woman, her tag identifying her as Claudia Rushmount, Nurse Practitioner, carried on with her kind smile but professional tone.

"He's been asked to oversee the cancer trial," she told me, "since he was one of the original researchers. He'll be checking in with you, I assure you, but he asked me to guide you through these next steps in your testing. If you have any questions, he said he'd make himself available."

Grumble, grump. "Okay," I said, even though it really wasn't. "What's next?"

Wouldn't you know? She carried on with her own private questions and examinations that felt far too much like a repeat of what I went through yesterday. At least this time I was a) talking to another woman and b) used to the invasion of privacy so that I could answer this time without all the stumbling and blushing. It also meant, as the more physical side of the exam took place, I was able to free my mind to go elsewhere.

Namely, to the conversation I'd overheard between Che and the cancer researcher and how Ian Linder was now likely spinning on his morgue slab knowing the doctor he'd tried to remove from the trial was now running it. But why had he tried to cut Che out of the project? Succeeded, even. Did that mean Che wasn't qualified to run it? Or because Che knew Ian wasn't playing straight? Didn't matter, I suppose, and was out of my hands for the time being. Because now that Linder was dead it looked like the whole shebang was in Dr. Che Mantegna's wheelhouse, capable or otherwise.

Why did I feel more confident in his management than the dead man's, despite knowing Ian Linder wanted Che out of the way? Probably for that very reason. Had I jumped to a conclusion I shouldn't have? It was like me, I admitted it to myself if never to anyone else (looking at you, Crew Turner). Still, this was Bernice's health and I honestly thought Che was the better doctor. But was he the better researcher?

I needed more information, obviously. And had to finally accept Che's takeover of a trial he'd just been kicked out of hours before his partner turned rival was found dead by yours truly? Sounded like an excellent motive for murder to me. Unless, of course, the trial was a fraud and a hoax. Did Che take over a dud? Should I warn him? Or was he in the know and had been the duper instead of the dupee (were those even words?) and had killed Ian Linder to hide the truth of the trial's fakery?

My brain was as tired of thinking as it was answering questions about my sex life, thanks. There were just too many variables to balance and not enough information to go on. And since I wasn't allowed to carry on the way I usually did because I made a mess (cue sarcastic resentment), we would be no closer to those answers by the time our excuse for being here ran out if my husband had any say in the matter.

Grumble, mumble.

I thanked Claudia as I left, so wrapped up in what I'd been thinking about I barely registered the fact Crew exited his own exam room and met up with me in the hall, the two of us making a short walk of our return to my room where I filled him in on Che's new position.

"I know," my husband said in the most annoyingly condescending (okay, his normal tone but I was still irked) ever. "We're thinking the same things, Fee." I looked for something to grouse about in that sentence as he went on. "If Che Mantegna is involved in the fraudulent trial, he could have killed Ian Linder to shut him up." I wanted to protest, because of the two doctors the former was far more my choice of innocent than the latter, but I held my tongue as Crew paced. "Then again, if Che found out Ian was cooking the trial, it's possible he lost his temper, and the death was an act of passion."

"Do we have confirmation on COD?" I was sure I did, thanks to my own exam, but if he wanted to play by the book suddenly, fine and dandy.

"Nothing from Liz or John," Crew said. Paused. "We could try to find out through Lloyd Aberstock."

"I thought you wanted to keep him in the dark." Oh, did you hear the sarcasm in those words? It was there, trust me on that and then some.

Crew's quick frown told me it was far from lost on him, either. "I want to protect our friends from information that they don't need to know until they need to know it."

"Until you need them in turn for something," I shot back. "You're not so worried about Lloyd's state of mind when you think you can use him to get to his brother. Because that's the plan, right, Crew?" Oh, I knew him so well, saw him flinch ever so slightly, the heat in his cheeks rise while his frown turned decidedly scowl-like. "Have Lloyd call Martin to contact the ME here and inquire about COD?" He didn't comment, hands on his hips, silent stare all the response I needed. "Meanwhile, I can tell you someone strangled Ian Linder to death with some kind of thin ligature (my mind went to his computer cord, the same one I'd tripped over, dangling, unplugged, from the wall), before said strangler stuffed the good doctor's mouth full of pills—to either deflect from their true identity or out of fury over the trial."

Crew waited a long moment before nodding. "I'll accept that."

Argh, what was all this conflict anyway? It had been a long time since we'd struggled like this. In fact, since we last had a case together, right? Maybe I needed to accept the fact my husband had his way of doing things and I had mine and never the twain should investigate the same job if marital bliss was the expected outcome.

"Let's run the scenario," Crew said then. "If Che killed Ian over the trial, it could have been motivated by sheer rage, right? Being cut out of a successful cancer research grant—and a possible cure—could mean a lot of money and prestige lost."

Agreed. "And if Che found out Ian was defrauding patients, that he was fired because of it, he might have killed Ian to protect those patients."

"Except," Crew said, one finger rising, his tone a little bit too much mansplaining for my liking, "if he did find out the drug was a fraud and killed Ian over it, why take over the trial? Why not expose it and Ian?"

Okay, fine, that was fair. "Then the other possibility is that Che is the one who was messing with the trial and Ian found out. That's why he kicked Che off the program and in order to protect himself, Che killed him." I didn't like it, not a bit, didn't buy it. But it had to be said out loud.

My husband's disbelief mirrored mine, at least. "Let's see what Liz found out. There's a good possibility we're not even in the right ballpark looking at Che."

That at least I could get behind.

"In the meantime." Crew drew a deep breath before holding his hands out to me. I took them, hesitant but feeling calmer, not so antagonistic, even though that possibility continued to simmer under my surface. "Why don't we split up," he said. Flinched after he said it. "For the case," he added in a hurry. I didn't tell him the caveat wasn't necessary, though the fact the slip bothered him had me troubled, too. Was he actually thinking we were that easy to break apart? Did I have something I needed to worry about? "We'll divide and conquer," he said.

"See what you can uncover with that clever nose of yours and I'll do the same."

I almost shot him down with a snarky comment about me and messes and why I should stay in the room like a good little Fleming and not be my busybody self, but honestly? I was already tired of fighting with him, and I just wanted this to be over so we could go home and never work together on a case again.

So, instead, I nodded and watched him go after he landed a soft and tentative kiss to my cheek, holding back a minute before exiting the room myself and heading for the dining room. Not with any specific destination in mind, but to grab a coffee and try to settle my mind.

Imagine my increased annoyance when I realized there was no coffee. I'd failed to notice at breakfast, too worked up about the dead doctor to pay attention. The best I could do was tea. Tea. Plain, green tea, no less.

Fine.

Are you as sick of that word as I was by then? Thought so.

I was just returning with my cup of sadness and disappointment when I spotted Brooke Poplar leaning over Sandra Linder in the outside garden, the view of the nurse saying something to the widow before she patted her on the shoulder and exited drawing me like a moth to a flame.

Nose at the ready, I entered the garden with one goal in mind. To show Crew Turner I wasn't just good at my job, I could do it without disaster, mayhem and death.

If only I believed that.

CHAPTER FOURTEEN

S HE SPOTTED ME AS I approached, though I wasn't exactly sneaking up on her. I half expected Sandra to bolt out of my presence. Instead, she slumped into the back of the bench, a veritable invitation for me to sit next to her and offer my sympathies. Which I did in that murmuring and lowered voice one used with the recently bereaved.

Sandra patted my free hand, the other of mine busy cradling my cup of green grief (absent all joy and hope in life without coffee. Okay, I'll stop, but come *on.*).

"Thank you, dear," she said. "You're so kind. Everyone is being so kind." Sandra burst into tears again, both hands now rising to cover her face. "I just wanted him to love me. To pay me the kind of attention he paid his stupid research." She almost spit that last word as her grief turned to vitriol and back again in a whip-crack of emotional turmoil that put what I'd been experiencing to shame. No matter how hard things were, someone always had it worse, right? "And now he's gone, and he'll never love me the way I wanted him to." Her wailing admission was as heartbreaking as it was horrifying, and I quickly hugged her, setting aside my rapidly cooling and unwanted tea of despair (I'm done, I swear) to do so.

"I'm sure he loved you," I said. "Some men just have a hard time expressing it." Some men, but not Crew, fortunately. Sigh. That was the first kind thing I'd thought about him since last night. I really did need to figure out what was wrong with me before I said something truly awful to him I couldn't take back. If I hadn't already. My mind raced in vague panic back over everything I'd said as Sandra went on, oblivious to my moment of *oh, crap*.

"What's it all been for?" She dropped her hands into her lap with two dull thuds as though they suddenly weighed far more than she was capable of supporting. "I did all of this just to get him to love me and for nothing. Nothing." Again with the weeping. While I found myself returning to her and the present after a quick scan of everything I could remember saying. And while yes, I'd been a bit prickly (hey, I don't need you judging me right now) I knew he loved me and would forgive me like I would forgive him (so there) for being kind of thoughtless in how he treated me. When I was his partner, not his assistant.

Whoops, there I went again, back on the bitterness train, chugging out of the station. I jerked hard on the brakes as she spun deeper into her own resentment.

"What am I going to do now?" Sandra spun on me, though it was obvious she wasn't asking me, not really. "After all of this, all the time I wasted, all the—" she halted her words abruptly, paling out to almost transparent, blinking through her tears. "I did everything I could to make him see me and I still wasn't enough. I wasted so much on him." Before I could stop her, she stood and bolted, far faster than a woman in her medical state should have been capable, let alone a healthy person. I was so shocked by her sudden exodus I just stared as she ran, not sure what that was all about but with a weird, uncomfortable feeling in my middle that I'd missed something important.

Whatever it was, I'd figure it out. I always did.

I almost left my tea behind but, with a sigh of irritation Mom raised me better than that, I fetched the cup, emptying the contents into the base of a tree I was sure could use the fluid, then headed back to the dining room to return it. I even put it in the dishwasher, you're welcome, the lack of staff about likely due to the lingering police presence. It was probable we'd all be interviewed at some point, and I needed to figure out what I was going to say beyond, I was in bed when the man died. Because I wasn't and lying didn't always work out the best for me.

All of that went away as I circled the work counter, heading for the main door to the dining room from the kitchen. The sound of two women talking had me stopping in my tracks and tucking up against the wall, peeking through the partially opened doorway where Lauren Sigler and Taylor Dulle had thought they'd found a quiet place out of the way to talk.

"I told you it was a fraud, and here's the proof." Taylor handed over a file to Lauren who slipped it quickly into the open top of her big, leather bag, nodding. "The pills, as promised." Lauren accepted the bottle, frowning as she shook the contents.

"You said you could get me a full prescription," the FDA investigator said. "There are only a few pills in here."

"I had to be careful," Taylor said, face pinched and pale. "The medication is carefully guarded, and the amounts checked and rechecked. You know how this works. If Ian suspected I was on to him, he would have taken steps to hide his fraud. This was the best I could do."

"I'm glad you followed through," Lauren said, finally depositing the pills into her bag as well, hefting it higher on her shoulder. "With Ian gone, the trial should be easy enough to stop."

"Exactly," Taylor said, taking a half-step closer. Lauren didn't seem comfortable with the change in proximity, but the drug rep didn't retreat. "As soon as Che has time to review all of the cases, I'm sure you'll have all the proof you need—aside from those," she jabbed a finger at Lauren's bag which the investigator tucked against herself in a protective manner. "Ian's recklessness put a lot of people at risk. My company just wants to be sure his arrogance doesn't impact other trials."

"Your company?" Lauren's instant discomfort mirrored my own, because hang on a second but wasn't Taylor's involvement—and being the investigator's source of suspicion against Dr. Linder—kind of self-serving? Like, not kind of, but big-time majorly a conflict of interest? Was Lauren just putting that together herself?

"Of course, I'm acting on my own," Taylor reassured her with the slick and smooth delivery of a born saleswoman which only made me suspect her more. "But you know Divinity Chemical is right now in process of administering our own cancer trial. The last thing we want is for the public's opinions to sour because some rogue doctor with an agenda and delusions of grandeur decided to fudge his research."

Lauren nodded but looked a bit sick, truth be told. "Of course," she said. "Thank you for this. I have to go." She hurried away from Taylor, past the doors and heading for the main offices, while Taylor watched her leave with a satisfied smirk before striding off for the interior of the building.

Whether she'd acted out of conscience or as a means to forward her own company's trial, one thing was clear to me. Taylor Dulle could not be trusted, and I needed to see what was in that file.

Which meant I followed Lauren Sigler as quickly

as I could without drawing attention to myself, relieved to find her stalled in her attempt to exit by none other than Phyllis Haines. The administrator had stopped weeping, at least, though she seemed intent on whatever it was she talked to Lauren about. In fact, she tugged the FDA investigator behind the counter of one of the nurse's stations, the pair whispering between them, leaving Lauren's big, leather bag exposed to a walk-by Fleming.

Pickpocketing, you say, aghast at the idea? Why, yes, I did stoop so low.

Paid off, too, don't you know.

CHAPTER FIFTEEN

I T WAS SURPRISINGLY EASY to liberate the file, and, to my delight, the pill bottle as well. As Lauren leaned toward Phyllis, I closed the distance and, with a quick hand dip, felt the smooth side of the plastic case brush my fingertips. With one casual motion, I had the bottle and the folder in my possession and was carrying on before anyone could notice, the women's washroom door beckoning me across the corridor.

And now you're wondering where I learned to lift things that didn't belong to me without the rightful owners knowing I'd done so. There was something to be said about spending afternoons in Irish pubs with silver-haired, blue-eyed criminal godfathers, drinking free beer, talking about the old country and learning new skills that impressed him so much even Malcolm Murray was shocked and appalled. Before laughing his head off at my natural ability to steal other people's property.

But I digress.

Once inside, I took the last stall and sat on the back of the toilet with my feet on the seat, my phone rapidly photographing the interior of the file and all its contents before I carefully shuffled them back into place and closed the folder over. That left liberating a pill from the bottle, though when I looked inside, I hesitated. There were only four. Would Lauren notice? I took the chance, slipping one of the large, blue pills free and tucking it into my pocket wrapped in toilet paper before resealing the bottle and hopping down.

Now to return the goods without Lauren noticing they'd been gone. That was going to prove harder to do than liberating them, it turned out. Malcolm only taught me how to take things, not put them back. My arrogance notwithstanding, I assumed I could simply reverse engineer the act and, presto magico, Bob's your uncle.

Which meant, as I was already congratulating myself on a quick and efficient job well done, my hand reaching out to slide the folder and bottle back into Lauren's still-gaping purse, she leaned back from Phyllis, their conversation over, and bumped into me.

Knocking the folder out of my hand and sending the bottle spinning away.

I did the only thing I could do in a haze of panic,

grasping for Lauren as if I'd tripped, tugging hard on the strap of her bag and, before she could complete her turn, jerking it free, scattering the contents over the floor.

"I'm so sorry!" I hit my knees to help her gather her things, Phyllis rushing to assist as well, the administrator frowning when she fetched the bottle though Lauren took it from her with a snatching motion that surprised Phyllis into silence.

"It's all right." Lauren stuffed her things back into her bag, flushed and embarrassed. "Accidents happen." She turned then and strode off, heading for the lobby and the exit, while my heart started beating again and my ridiculously childish ego did a jig of joyful success that we'd gotten away with it.

Crew would be so *pissed*.

If I told him. Which was still under debate.

I hurried back to my room and called Daisy, my husband nowhere to be found. Which made it easier to tell my bestie and the newest employee of Fleming Investigations what I'd done and what I'd found.

"I'm sending you the pictures of the file," I said.

"I'll take a look right now," she told me. "What are you going to do about the pills?"

I hesitated a moment, pondering the question. I really didn't have many options. And made a decision that would, yet again, make my husband very angry if and when (oh, when, come on now) he found out. "Lloyd Aberstock," I said. "He'll know if they are authentic."

"Great idea," she gushed. At least someone was

on my side. I had to bite back the temptation to dump on Daisy, to unearth all the awful things I'd been thinking and feeling about Crew and myself. Not that she'd have minded because she was the best bestie whoever bestied and I literally could have told her I was the murderer and she'd have offered to help me hide the body. Because that was my Daisy Bruce. But she didn't need to deal with what was clearly my problem while I was on a job and I had to focus, darn it. Maybe when I got home over a bottle of chardonnay or that fruity white Gewürztraminer she loved. For now, I had a job to do, and I was finally doing it, so no distractions could be allowed in the way.

Not even Crew Turner.

It was a quick and productive walk to the Aberstocks for two reasons. One, I managed to lift my own spirits with the previous reassurance I was on the case and had things to do and people to suspect and progress to report at last. That kind of forward motion—not just the feet moving kind—always made me feel optimistic. My successful foray into the illegal activities I'd learned at my godfather's knee had me a little giddy, I admit. Even better, however, when I knocked on the door and Lloyd answered, he was alone, which meant I felt free to unload whatever I knew without fear his lovely wife would be adversely affected.

Oh, I had an excuse for everything, trust me.

"Bernice is at an appointment," he said. "You have something to tell me she shouldn't hear." Not a question. The man really was brilliant.

"I have a lot to tell you," I said, "that Crew and Dad want me to stay quiet about." Yeah, I had to go and rat them out, right?

But Lloyd was Lloyd and chuckled. "Of course, they did," he said. "They're looking out for me, Fee, like they look out for you and everyone else they love. I understand. I've been in on their silence myself." He cleared his throat, blinked quickly as tears rose. "It's far different being on this side of the quiet, though."

He could say that again. Rather than linger over my own nasty history with their lack of information sharing, I held up the two pills, now in their own separate baggies, and offered them to him.

Lloyd took them in his hands, turning them over, before meeting my eyes with his blue ones full of questions. "Where did you get the trial meds, Fee?"

"So, these are a match to what Bernice is taking." Okay, I had that much confirmed at least.

"They look to be," he said. "I can't confirm that without a chemical analysis, however. If you came by them outside of the trial's dosing protocol, you would have to compare them to an original pill in order to confirm their authenticity. But even that's risky since the chemical makeup of the drug is proprietary. Anyone caught running an analysis by the FDA risks serious fines and even possible loss of employment."

"We'll burn that bridge when we find someone to build it," I said.

He laughed. Long and loud and with tears in his eyes and breathlessness that ended in a gasping catch of air. "I've always loved how you think, Fee." Lloyd finally turned then from my open grin and went to Bernice's side table. There, he opened a drawer, fishing out a small box. When he returned to me, it was with a guilty look on his face that had me groaning.

"I'm not the only thief," I said.

He showed me half a pill he'd somehow managed to scrounge, wrapped tightly in a strip of what looked like plastic wrap. "It was Bernice's first dose," he said. "I was unsure even then. I figured a half a pill at the beginning wouldn't hurt. I always intended to take it home and test it myself, but we haven't left and she's so much better." He seemed to hesitate before he handed it firmly to me to add to my collection. "You have someone to do the testing?"

I didn't, but I knew someone who might. "Leave it to me," I said.

"And stay out of it," Lloyd said. Grimaced. "Right?"

I paused then, biting my lower lip, hating that was exactly what I was suggesting. Because didn't Dad do it to me, Crew? Lloyd wasn't some hysterical client with a vendetta or a paranoia problem. He was Dr. Aberstock and of anyone I trusted, he was top of the list. So, why was it so easy to fall in line now that I had what I wanted and needed to carry on?

I was not that person. It took me all of five minutes to fill him in on everything I knew, including things Crew didn't yet, so there, Captain Handsompants FBIGuy DoAsISayer.

Lloyd accepted everything I told him with a level stare before hugging me tightly when I was done. "Thank you," he whispered, choked up. "I promise I'll keep this to myself. But I need to know, Fee. I really do."

I understood that so hard I almost broke. "You always did the same for me," I said, also a bit weepy, truth be told.

"Not always, Fee," he said, letting me go. "There were times I listened when they wanted me to stay quiet. And I did. I'm so sorry for that."

"You did what you thought was right," I told him. "And so am I. All that matters right now?" He nodded. "Bernice is going to be okay, Lloyd. Because of you."

He was blinking furiously as I left, though it was hard to see that while tears trailed from my own eyes.

CHAPTER SIXTEEN

I MADE A CALL the moment I returned to my room, though honestly, I wasn't holding out much hope for success. To my surprise, the cheerful woman on the other end immediately offered assistance despite Dr. Aberstock's previous warning.

"This is Lloyd and Bernice," Penny Keene said, the Curtis County ME assistant not even hesitating when I broached the subject. "And you're in luck, Fee. I might know the perfect guy. Hang on, I'll call you back." She hung up without further ado, leaving me to message Daisy with my updates. It wasn't long before Penny's name showed up on my screen, her happy voice informing me what she'd done.

"David will meet you in the parking lot of the

clinic in a half-hour," she said. "White sedan, Rhode Island plates. He'll be wearing a blue ballcap, fully bearded and mustached."

Wow, that was quick. "I take it there's a story here?" I hurriedly nabbed the welcome package we'd received, liberating the envelope the brochures came in, sliding the pills inside and sealing it as Penny chuckled.

"Well, sort of," she said. "We went to school together. Dave's kinda got a crush on me. And he owes me a big favor. He's discreet," she sobered as she went on, "and he knows this is important to me. He has access to a private lab and promised to take care of it ASAP."

"Thanks, Penny," I said.

"Hug Lloyd and Bernie for me," she said. "Oh, and if David asks if I'm single, tell him I have a boyfriend, please?" Her pleading tone had me grinning. "Little white lie, but I'd hate to hurt him."

That had me wondering, as I made the promise and hung up, what happened between her and Rowan Mallory. The last time we'd worked a case together—was that just a few weeks ago?—Daisy had pointed out the clear attraction Penny had for the rumpled and brilliant homicide specialist. I'd gotten the impression Penny was ready to make a move in that regard. Had she failed to do so? Or had Mallory (foolishly) turned her down? Whatever the case, while it really wasn't any of my business, I'd be asking her pointed questions when I got home. Because since when were other people's secrets a reason for me to mind my own?

Crew didn't show up before David's quick text alerted me he was on time, so rather than trouble my husband and make us look even more conspicuous by having the two of us deliver the goods to the young tech, I took it upon myself to exit the side door and circle to the back of the building in the now dim afternoon as clouds rolled in to smother the sunlight and give the world a distinctive gloom I hoped wasn't foreshadowing and just natural phenomenon.

It was easy enough to spot the white sedan and blue-capped, dark-bearded driver, Penny's friend parked off to one side, engine running. He looked rather nervous when I handed him the envelope despite the fact no one approached or even seemed to notice he was there.

"Thank you," I said, handing him one of my cards. "If you could call me with the results, David...?" I hesitated, suddenly aware Penny hadn't told me much about him of an informational nature while telling me oodles of personal.

He flinched, tugging his cap down over his dark sunglasses, snatching the envelope from me and slamming the car into gear, even as his window hummed shut. "No last names." And, with that, he drove off at a rather erratic pace while I shrugged and headed back inside. Not that asking someone to risk their career over a case was a small thing, but he clearly hadn't had much experience with anything clandestine in the past.

Penny was a horrible influence.

I was almost to the corner of the building when I heard the back door open and the sound of footfalls hurrying out into the parking lot. That had me dodging behind a bush, even as another car spun onto the scene, this one a big, black sedan. It pulled up and parked in front of Phyllis Haines, the woman stopping in her tracks as the back door opened and a man gestured to her. I watched Phyllis hesitate before she approached, hunching over and having a quiet conversation with whoever it was who'd arrived. A moment later, she slipped something out of her purse, glancing over her shoulder at the door—and missing my presence, fortunately, while I jerked out my phone and filmed, just in time, as he accepted what she offered, a narrow envelope disappearing into her bag as the door to the car slammed shut and the driver moved off. I zoomed in just in time, caught the plate as they drove off, while Phyllis hesitated before spinning and marching back inside the clinic.

Well now. What was that all about? Not hard to recognize a trade-off when I saw one, and more than likely illegal, if the envelope Phyllis now carried was full of the cash my brain said was the most logical contents. Sure, I didn't have proof of that. For all I knew it was a totally innocuous exchange. Maybe it was Crew's earlier accusations about my leaps of judgment and intuition that had me hesitating to trust my gut like I usually did. Whatever the reason, my self-doubt didn't stop me from forwarding the plate to Liz.

Can you find out who this car belongs to? It really annoyed me I suddenly felt like I was going behind Crew's back contacting her like this, despite the fact, technically, she worked for me. I knew it wasn't his fault, but I couldn't help but blame his previous observations (I use that term generously) had me discombobulated and wondering if he was right.

She texted back immediately. *Will do.*

At least she didn't seem to think I was a wild card who ran off half-cocked and needed to be more careful. No, that's not what Crew said, I get that. Implied it, though, didn't he? And my agile and awful brain filled in the gaps because it was awesome like that.

As distracted as I was by my return to emotional spiraling, I failed to realize Crew had returned to my (*our*—my continuing use of the singular pronoun wasn't lost on me) room until I was already inside, head down over my phone while I forwarded the video I'd taken to Daisy.

I looked up to find my handsome, darling husband was glaring back at me, arms crossed over his chest, visibly agitated with that broad jaw of his jumping, the fake glasses discarded, all Crew Freaking Turner watching my return with, yet again, that old antagonism I'd thought we'd left behind us when he quit his job as sheriff of Reading.

"Where have you been?" Wait, wasn't he the one who said we should go our separate ways? I didn't get to argue the point when he waved off my attempt, tsking softly under his breath. "Never mind," he said, shaking his head, staring at the floor now, hands back on his hips, stance solid and almost rigid. "I had my doubts about this, Fee," he said. "About working together. And now I'm wishing I'd listened to myself." He met my eyes with his own blue ones troubled. "We'll talk about it when we get home." Crew dropped his hands to his sides, body relaxing into a more casual stance that lied about his continuing tension. I knew him better than that, could still see it tugging at the corners of his eyes, the lines of his mouth. Someone else might have missed it, thought him the epitome of confident coolness, but this was my husband and I'd set him off more than enough times over the years he couldn't fool me.

Funny, I never really tried to fool him. Why he felt the need to hide from me I wasn't sure. Oh, and the fact he shut me down without allowing me to respond or join the conversation? You better believe that was going to be part of the conversation he decided unilaterally to carry out when we got back to Reading. We'd just see how one-sided that talk (oh, there would be yelling, too, trust me) ended up once we were done here.

We'd just *see*.

"What did you find out?" Crew's tone was, at least, level and composed and carried zero emotional weight, so he clearly wasn't interested in triggering me further.

High road? I'd take it, for now. "Let's read in the

whole team," I said. We really did need to catch them up and besides, having the rest of Fleming Investigations on the call might keep the two of us from devolving into fighting again.

Right then? I'd have paid a lot to stop fighting with Crew.

CHAPTER SEVENTEEN

IT ONLY TOOK A moment to get everyone on the line, the sound of Dad saying something to Mom before a door closing behind him shut out the sound of the TV the final addition to the conference call. I quickly filled everyone in on what I'd discovered, stumbled over and, without missing a beat, had chosen to tell Lloyd Aberstock. As I unfolded the details I'd uncovered, it surprised me just how much had happened in the few short hours I'd been digging around, privately pleased with myself. Not that the bulk of it hadn't been luck, mind you, but still.

"Nice job, Fee," Daisy said, broke the silence that fell when I ground to a halt. "I did as you asked and looked into Lauren Sigler. She checks out, has an excellent record with the FDA. I spoke to her secretary, Kimmy, who said she's even had a couple of commendations." Leave it to Daisy to find a way to connect with a source who would talk to her. "Kimmy also said Lauren lost her mother to cancer three years ago and that she has a serious focus on trials like this one since her mom took part in one, but it didn't save her."

"Good to know," I said. "Great work, Day." I could picture her dimples as she grinned in the office at home, but it wasn't false praise. "If she really was emotionally connected to the trial's outcome, if she found out for sure Ian Linder was a fraud, it sounds like she had motive for manslaughter, at the very least."

"And she was there last night," Crew said. "So, she's on the suspect list. For the detective." He shot me a look. "What do we know about the trial? Anything to help our clients?"

Oh, he did *not* just shoot me down in front of everyone. Yes, okay, fine, the dead doctor wasn't my job or my case, the Aberstocks were. And, come *on*. Sigh.

"I looked into Taylor Dulle," Liz said, her level tone taking over the line. "According to my source in the FBI, she's been taken to task a couple of times for challenging patents without cause. She's a real piece of work, from what I found out, but nothing actionable. There was even an accusation of corporate espionage against her last year, but the charge was dropped for lack of evidence."

"That paperwork Fee sent me," Daisy said. "Liz, I forwarded it to you. Did you get it?"

"I didn't," she said, "hang on." There was a moment of silence then tapping keys. "Got it, Day, thanks. Yeah, looks like she managed to get her hands on some records from the trial." Liz's voice trailed off a moment. "Huh. According to this, Linder was definitely fudging his numbers. Looks like he was skewing the results to make the drug look more successful than it really is."

I felt my heart sink, even as Day spoke up again, voice tentative. "Could she have falsified the documents?" I hadn't thought of that, paused and pondered it as Liz chuckled. "Sorry," Daisy blurted then. "Never mind, it's a silly idea."

"I was about to say it's brilliant," Liz said. "Don't ever apologize, Daisy. I'll look into this further, but you're right. It's possible she did just that. Might have upped her game, especially since she's been known to try to throw wrenches into other people's research for her own company's gain. You do know they are running their own trial, based on similar research?"

"She mentioned as much to Lauren," I said.

"Stands to reason she'd want this trial to fail," Dad said.

"Let me see what my source says," Liz said. "Day, can you coordinate with me on this? I want your mind in on it. I like how you think."

Daisy spluttered a moment before responding. "Of course," she said. "I'm happy to help, Liz." I fought a grin, glad she couldn't see it, proud of my amazing friend. And grateful to Liz for doing what I never seemed to be able to—convince Daisy she was awesome.

"Great," Liz said with uncharacteristic enthusiasm. "Anything else come up?"

"I looked at Dr. Che Mantegna," Dad said then, whisper of shuffling papers over the line as the old-school investigator in him looked at what was likely a stack of pages he could have easily read from the computer. The eco-friendly woman in me winced but didn't comment because it wouldn't do a lick of good. "Turns out he was part of a lawsuit against Linder last year. He worked with the victim for ten years on this very project, was part of it from the start, but quit three years ago, only signing back on a year before the case he leveled against Linder."

"Why did Che turn against him?" I remembered vividly their argument as Dad responded.

"Looks like Mantegna's story is similar to Lauren Sigler's," he said. "Except instead of his mother, it was his wife who died. She was in the original trial he and Linder ran for the drug Bernice is taking now."

Yikes. "Was he suing Linder?"

"I have the suit details, John," Jill piped up, reminding me she was there. "Che Mantegna claimed that Ian Linder used only placebos in that trial, that he refused to test the drug itself but didn't want to lose his funding. According to the lawsuit, Mantegna had multiple patients tested for the drug and none of them had it in their system. But Linder had backing from the FDA who vetted his research—their research—and the suit didn't go anywhere."

"There's no way he should be running the trial now," Crew said, elbows on his knees, hands clasped before him, frowning at them.

"His claim was honored by the FDA," Liz said. "He had proof the drug's design was his in the first place." It was? "He only handed it over yesterday morning after the body was found."

"That's not a bit suspicious, is it?" I let out a long sigh. "What are we thinking here?"

"Not enough information yet," Dad said. "But it's pretty clear Che Mantegna had motive for murder, as did Lauren Sigler."

"I have something," Kit piped up, the youngest of our number jumping into the fray. "Liz had me run down that license plate of yours, Fee." Phyllis's clandestine connection? "It's registered to a shell corporation out of New York. But I managed to track it to its parent company. Something called Parson BioChem."

"No way," Liz said while Crew sat up straighter. "It can't be."

"The plot thickens," Dad said.

"Does it ever," Crew growled. "Nero Parson isn't a researcher or a drug company exec like his corp name suggests."

"He's a black-market smuggler of prescription drugs," Liz said, almost sounding happy. "Mostly expensive, experimental drugs."

"How is he involved?" Crew sat back then, frowning. "I didn't think we'd ever get anything on him, Liz. Not after leaving the Bureau."

"Tell me about it." She was almost gleeful. "I'll get in touch with the New York field office and see what they can tell us. This would be a coup, Turner. A freaking *coup*." She laughed then, a rarity for Liz. While my husband's continuing frown tempered the whole conversation.

"One more thing," I said, thoughts about my marriage bringing up another one that was much more unhappy than mine even in my present state. "What do we know about Sandra Linder?" I almost stopped myself, but something about our conversation lingered with me, had me frowning, too, just like Crew.

"I'll take that," Kit piped up.

"Find out how long she's been sick," I said. "What she has, specifically." What had she said? Something about doing everything she could to make him see her, that it still wasn't enough. Why did it ring oddly to me in retrospect?

"On it," she said.

"Well done, gang," Dad said. "And while I do agree with Crew, our focus is the Aberstocks, if we can hand the police a win on murder, I'm not against it." The group murmur of agreement had my back up instantly, made worse by the flash of something I didn't recognize on my husband's face. "Speaking of which, we haven't heard from you yet," Dad said. "What about you, Crew?"

Why did my father's question feel like a stake through my heart?

CHAPTER EIGHTEEN

OKAY, I'LL ADMIT IT. There was more than a modicum of professional pride involved here, especially considering the way Crew had been treating me since we started this case (or how I perceived him treating me, I'd give him the benefit of the doubt for now). Which had me suddenly uncomfortable and nervous. What had I really done, then? I'd bumbled about, ran into trouble and out again, tripped my way over things that may or may not have had anything to do with the case at hand, and gave the team not a whole heck of a lot, truth be told. At least, that's what my traitor ego whispered to me as I tensed next to my husband, waiting for him to drop a giant bombshell like he'd single-handedly caught the murderer in action and forced them to confess while saving a family from a burning house and rescuing a kitten from a tree.

Fee. That was so beneath you.

To my surprise, Crew grunted something under his breath before sighing. "I haven't been able to get access to Linder's office," he said, frustration coming through just enough I caught the edges of it. "I'm working on it."

"While you do that," Dad said, "let's address the elephant in the room, shall we?" An electric sizzle of *oh my god*, what raced through me, panic punching me in the chest, as Dad went on, oblivious to the fact he just gave his only daughter heart failure as I lurched over what he was about to say. "The Aberstocks do not need to be drawn into this mess any further than they are." That was aimed at me, but it was lost on me at the moment, honestly, because I was busy picking up the panicked pieces of my trauma. "Can we agree to hold off telling them anything further until we know for certain if the trial is a fraud or not?"

Okay, that brought me back. "What if the drugs Bernice is taking are killing her, Dad?" I let out a quick breath in irritation when Crew drew one of his own. "Yes, fine, she looks great. Still. We're here for *them*, aren't we?" Never mind I was on the road to recovery from a near-hysterical crash into the belief Dad was about to confront me over, what? Fighting with Crew? Demand to know why we weren't working together like good little investigators? Dig into my private thoughts and unearth my internal battle? An utterly illogical assumption pit my ego tried to throw me into, one I'd barely clawed my way out of while trying to assemble a rational argument. All while being totally irrational inside.

"For all we know," Dad said at his level best, "the drug is perfectly fine, Taylor Dulle has been sowing seeds of doubt for her company's benefit and Bernice Aberstock is actually on her way to a full recovery thanks to the trial. But even if the result is otherwise, Fee, it's irresponsible for us to divulge anything we're uncovering in the course of this investigation, even to someone like Lloyd Aberstock, without concrete proof."

Grumble.

Growl.

Mumble.

"Fine."

Just *fine*. Not.

That ended the conversation, Dad the last to hang up. "I know you, Fiona Fleming," he said. "Your loyal heart is at war with itself. I love you for it. But do Lloyd and Bernice a favor and stop including them." He let us go then, Crew standing the moment Dad was off the line, pacing away from me, hands now deep in his pockets.

"Dinner," I said, glancing at my phone, feeling dull and sullen despite the fact I'd single-handedly forwarded our investigation on multiple fronts, thank you.

"Dinner," Crew said. And waited for me to join him, letting me walk ahead of him out the door.

It was quiet at the table, though Bernice did her

best to keep up the chatter. Even Lloyd seemed reserved and restrained, and I began to wonder if Dad had been right. Was my choice to include the normally jovial ME in what I'd uncovered acting to his detriment? I just couldn't bring myself to buy it, however. It was clear from the way he stared off into space from time to time Lloyd had a lot on his mind and had for some time. Likely since Bernice was diagnosed.

His reticence at dinner wasn't on me.

As for the lovely lady of the hour, she took note, it turned out, of the quiet between myself and my husband, and, when Crew finally excused himself after dinner, she reached out to take my hand and keep me with her while Lloyd exited with a soft kiss for her cheek and squeeze of my shoulder.

"I've known you since you were a little girl," she said, eyes bright and sparkling but with enough worry, I kicked myself for letting my issues get in the way when she was the one needing support. "And while I missed a decade of your life when you left Reading for New York, I feel like I still know the girl inside you." She let my hand go, kind smile as full of compassion and kindness as ever, cancer or no cancer. "You've always had that spunk and stubbornness I saw in Lucy, but with your father's determination and quick thinking. Honestly, I knew it would take a remarkable man to catch your eye and keep you, Fee." She glanced toward the entry to the dining room where Crew stood, in quiet conversation with Lloyd. "Did I tell you about the day I met him?"

For a moment, I thought she meant her husband until she giggled a bit and blushed. "Handsome Sheriff Crew Turner, brand new and still smiling, with that white hat of his and the way those jeans fit." I gasped a bit, caught my own breathless laugh, as Bernice snorted. "I'm an old lady, dear," she said with a raised eyebrow, "I'm not dead. Yet." She poked the back of my hand with one finger, winking, taking the edge from her words with that simple flutter of eyelashes. "My goodness, he made an impression in town. I worried about him, Fee, from day one. It was obvious to me, Crew had no idea what he'd walked into, coming to Reading, taking over from John that way. He had it so hard, and he bore it all with such grace." I nodded, swallowed the lump rising in my throat, stealing another peek at my husband. Where had my anger come from? Why was I annoyed with him again? Her voice softened everything as she went on. "I didn't think he'd last, honestly. And then in walks Fee Fleming, back from New York City with her flaming hair and her whirlwind presence, taking over Petunia's and our whole town by storm." Bernice laughed as I shook my head.

"You remember things differently than I do," I said. From what I recalled, I limped home, fresh from my breakup with my cheating ex, without a clue how to run the bed and breakfast I'd inherited from a grandmother with more secrets than anyone I'd ever known.

"I remember well enough," Bernice said. "That

boy," she nodded toward Crew, "took one look at you and decided to stay. No matter what."

"I made him crazy," I said.

"You made him love again." Bernice patted my hand, leaning closer. "Fee, dear. I've been married a long time and I've loved Lloyd since the day we met. I know love at first sight when I see it. And Crew had it." She shrugged. "You're going to have tough times," she said. "It happens. It's how you deal with conflict that defines your relationship, dear, not who wins. In the end, loving the person you're with enough to hear both sides, to accept that there are things you'll never change, and not wanting to, matters so much more than being right."

Inhale. Argument. Acceptance.

Yeah. Sigh.

I hugged her, retreated, thinking about what she'd said far more than the case. Found myself hanging out in the indoor garden, listening to the night crickets wake as darkness descended, the trickle of water from somewhere, the sigh of the leaves as a bit of a breeze made it down through the gap to the sky and rustled the very tops of the foliage. A few people came and went as I sat there and let my mind wander, but no one approached or bothered me until, suddenly tired, I stood and went back to our room—mine and Crew's—with a firm intention.

He was sitting on the bed with his back to the wall, on his phone, when I entered. Crew glanced up but didn't comment, quiet when I climbed up beside him and leaned my head against his shoulder.

"I'm sorry," I said. "I don't know why we're fighting, but I want to figure it out."

He set his phone aside, arms going around me. "I love you so much," he whispered. "You amaze me, Fiona Fleming." His chest rose and fell as he inhaled and exhaled a giant breath, body curving into mine, chin on the top of my head. "You make me crazy."

"I know," I said. "It's not the first time you said that." Why was I in the past again? Thinking about my return to Reading and our rocky beginning? Because Bernice brought it up? It felt like more than that.

"Won't be the last." He chuckled. "Wow, you really showed me up earlier."

I sat back, eyes wide, shaking my head as he grinned at me.

"I didn't mean to," I said. Sagged, guilty and lost. "You're right about me. I'm a mess. I stagger from one disaster to another, stumbling over other people's secrets like a bull in a china shop."

He tugged me to him again, hugging me tightly. "You get the job done," he said. "I think I was jealous."

He was...? I didn't get to protest.

"Listen," Crew said, "I've worked at this job my whole adult life. I've always wanted to be in law enforcement. But it never felt right until I started doing PI work. With you and your dad and this whole crazy setup you've sucked me and Liz and Jill into." His bemused tone was equally amused. "I know you come by it honestly. I've worked side-by-side with your dad long enough to admit it's a natural ability, not training, that drives him. And you, my love." Crew let me go when I pulled away again, to stare into his eyes as he finished. "Don't ever stop being you. Even if it puts you at risk. Even if I have to panic and have heart attacks on the regular when you throw yourself in the line of fire. Even if it means I'm an idiot to you sometimes and treat you horribly because my ego gets prickly and can't handle how awesome you are at this."

I wasn't sure what to say to that. "I've been awful to you for no reason," I finally blurted. "You're the best husband ever."

"Let's agree we're both jerks," he said, "and let it go?"

I hugged him, kissed him. Melted into him. Felt him melt into me, too.

"I wish," he growled in my ear as things got heated. "But I was hoping for a different kind of action from you, Mrs. Everett."

"That's a shame," I said, "Mr. Everett. What did you have in mind?"

"How about a lovely game of B&E?" He winked. "I hear you have a knack for getting into places you're not supposed to be and finding things you're not supposed to uncover."

"You say the sweetest things," I said, batting my lashes. "Shall we see what Dr. Ian Linder had to hide?"

His answering grin had me wishing he hadn't turned my first offer down.

CHAPTER NINETEEN

THIS TIME WHEN WE snuck our way into the offices, luck was with us. Without a soul around to interfere and the security cameras easily avoidable (laughable, honestly, which had me wondering if Phyllis arranged that on purpose to cover her own illegal activities), Crew and I entered Ian Linder's office with a short effort at picking the lock on my husband's behalf making my eyebrows arch.

He just grinned at me and let us inside, closing the door behind us and moving immediately to the filing cabinets. I squared my shoulders and took the desk again, the chair in which I'd last seen the researcher now vacant, his laptop missing but desktop present. I sat with ginger delicacy on the far front of the chair, trying not to think about the dead body who had previously occupied it, and booted up the PC.

This one, it seemed, was the property of the clinic and had been left behind, Dr. Linder's private computer taken by the police. Which meant I was likely out of luck looking for anything probative, but no stone unturned and all that.

We were thorough, make no mistake, but within ten minutes it was obvious to me there wasn't anything here to find. Crew turned to me as I clicked through the messy desktop's disorganized folders, hunkering down next to me and shaking his head.

Time to compare notes. Not many to compare, from the frustrated look on his face.

"I took photos of everything I could find," he said. "Nothing jumped out at me as shady. Anything on the computer?"

"Not a thing." I sighed and sat back, though one last folder remained to check, so I did so with less enthusiasm than I should have. "Unless he had separate files on his laptop," I said as I double-clicked, "it looks like Ian Linder was on the up and up."

"I'll send all of this to Liz," Crew said. "You're right, though. If he was going to keep separate files, they probably wouldn't be here."

"We had to check." I froze as the folder popped open, leaning in again with a burst of renewed energy. "I spoke too soon. Looks like these are the main test results." Which had my heart fluttering as I scanned down the list of names attached to folders embedded in the main file. Paused at Sandra Linder and clicked it. Crew leaned in as I caught my breath.

"She's cured." His voice actually held awe. We both sat back in stunned silence for a long moment before he spoke again. "You mean, it works?" Our gazes met, locked, hope making me smile in dazed surprise.

"Bernice," I said. And turned my attention back to the computer screen, scanning once again, but this time for a beloved name.

I didn't get to check. Crew hissed at me, tugging on my sleeve, the sound of whispering voices approaching so rapidly I'd missed them in my focus on the open folder and the possibility Bernice was in the right place after all. We barely had time to duck under the desk when the door opened and the two arguing people entered, their voices rising slightly, just enough I could identify them, while Crew and I stared into one another's eyes as Che Mantegna and Taylor Dulle entered the office and closed the door behind them.

"You said he was doctoring the results," Che said, anger a palpable thing in the air of the room, though it could have been my discomfort with being in a compromising position that gave me that sense of dread.

"There was evidence of that. I even shared with Lauren." Taylor's soothing tone might have worked to placate others, but Che wasn't having it.

"Proof you provided," he shot back. "I trusted

you on this, Taylor. And now I'm wondering if that was the right decision." Now I needed to check in with Liz and Day and see if they'd uncovered anything untoward because it certainly seemed like Che Mantegna had reason to doubt the folder she'd given the FDA investigator.

"We agreed we needed to act," she said, stressing the pronoun. "For the good of the trial and the patients." Her wheedling tone had my back up. "You were doing them a favor sabotaging the trial."

He did what? My eyes widened, Crew's too, while Che fell silent a moment.

"I've seen Ian's reports," he said then, dull and heavy. "The drug is working, Taylor."

She hissed something softly I missed before speaking again. "That's just a few aberrations."

"A sixty percent remission rate isn't an aberration," he said. "It's success, Taylor. And twenty percent of the remainder are seeing a marked reduction in cell growth. This is huge."

"You can't turn your back on me now," she snarled suddenly. "I have proof you've been tampering with the trial, Che. If you try to backstab me, I'll take you down."

His soft exhale sounded resigned. "So be it," he said. "I blamed Ian for Margaretta's death. I was sure he'd tampered with my formula." Che's formula? "But now I'm wondering if she'd had a little more time, if I hadn't been such a stubborn, blaming fool, would this new advancement have saved her." I could hear his voice thickening, his last two words warbling and cracked with emotion. Felt myself choke up for his sake.

Taylor, however, didn't seem to have an ounce of empathy. "Pull yourself together," she snarled. "You're in this up to your neck and I'm holding you to your promise." He grunted softly, but she went on before he could speak. "Did you kill him?"

Che gasped. "I certainly did not," he said. Paused. "Did you?"

Taylor actually laughed, filled with derision and disdain. "Please. Like I'd get my own hands dirty." I believed her in that moment, utterly. Because she was right and a person like her who manipulated others to do her bidding? No way she'd stoop to strangling someone herself.

Then again, was she believable?

"I'm done arguing about this," Taylor said, the sound of the doorknob turning and softly echoing sound of her voice fading indicating she was on her way out. "Either do what you promised and tank this trial, or I'll make sure you spend the rest of your professional life slinging fries." The sound of footfalls faded, followed by another deep sigh.

"I can't do that, Taylor," Che whispered, before he, too, exited, the door closing behind him.

"Well," Crew said after a long moment of waiting for distance to make it safe to speak, "that was interesting."

"And now we know for sure the source of the suspicion isn't valid," I said. "It's an attempt at sabotage."

"Let's get out of here," Crew said, sliding out from under the desk and offering his hand. He pulled me up next to him, hugging me quickly in a rush of what looked like delight on his face. "I get it," he said, while I cocked my head in confusion. "Why you love doing things your way. That was a rush." He chuckled while I shook my head at him.

"Breaking in here was your idea, Mr. Turner," I said.

"Maybe you're rubbing off on me," he said, booping my nose with one index finger.

My, how attractive he was in that moment, how delicious, really, with the surge of adrenaline from almost being caught swirling around with the exultation of uncovering evidence all comingling with the truly yumtasticness that was my husband.

Hormones aside, I have no idea what we might have gotten up to if the door to the office hadn't opened one more time. Brooke Poplar entered in a rush, eyes flying wide as she took in the two of us standing there, three shocked people all exchanging looks before the nurse pointed at us with anger flashing over her face.

"I knew it!" She shook her head, grim as she reached for her phone. "Neither of you are who you said you are and I'm calling the police."

Whoops.

CHAPTER TWENTY

I SAT NEXT TO my husband in Phyllis Haines's office while Crew explained who we were and why we were there. We'd agreed he was the right one to do the talking, not because I was known to run off at the mouth (no laughing), but because he had more experience talking people down than I did. And, when he mentioned the FBI? That made him an instant source of trust, though Phyllis did seem uncomfortable in his presence after that.

It had taken until morning before everyone was assembled sufficiently for Crew to do his charming best to keep us both from being arrested. The detective in charge of the homicide case, Bob Prouse, didn't seem all that interested in pressing charges and with Phyllis's reluctance to do so quickly stammered out when my husband told Prouse what we knew and why we were there, the detective instead warmed to both of us.

Well, Crew. And me by default.

But it wasn't just Phyllis and Prouse in the room at that point. Nope, things had gotten a little crowded since Brooke's shrieking and panicked phone call had brought the authorities. Lauren Sigler stood off in one corner, arms crossed over her chest, scowl of disbelief aimed at me and Crew, though she seemed less sure of herself when Crew told the detective there was no actionable evidence to prove Linder had been messing with his trial.

"In fact," my husband said, "we now have reason to believe the trial was being sabotaged from within and that there's an excellent chance the purpose was corporate espionage."

Lauren flinched at that. Glanced down at her big bag now sitting at her feet.

"Your clients could have alerted me to their concerns." Phyllis dabbed at her upper lip with a damp tissue, her tone huffy but the visible nervousness she fought cutting off her credibility, at least in my eyes.

Oh, that was the other thing we agreed to. We were keeping the Aberstocks out of it, if possible, though Brooke knew we were friends, so it was going to come out sooner or later. As long as it didn't keep Bernice from finishing the trial. "Our clients," Crew said, "had every reason to be concerned, it appears, Ms. Haines."

143

She didn't have anything to say to that.

"There's clearly a bigger issue here," Crew went on with smooth confidence. "I've already been in touch with my contacts in the Bureau as well as the FDA." Lauren twitched again. "And the question remains, did Dr. Linder's murder have anything to do with this attempt to sabotage his work and the trial."

"And my clinic," Phyllis squeaked.

Crew nodded graciously. "We'll have a thorough report for you, Ms. Haines," he said in that official and dreadful voice of his. "Areas of improvement in your security, for example. Your system is woefully inadequate. Any number of unsavory types could gain access without much effort." His blue eyes never left hers and I caught her moment of terror just before she smothered it.

She knew he knew about Nero Parson.

"Please, of course." She blurted that abruptly, standing and waving her limp tissue in Crew's direction. "I'm delighted to have, um," she looked down at her desk and the card Crew had presented her with a little while ago, "Fleming Investigations work for my clinic. *Delighted*. Thank you. Any insights would be appreciated." She spun on Prouse in haste with her hands shaking. "I'm just mortified, detective. How any of this could go on under my nose…"

"I'd like to see your evidence," Lauren said, face clouded with doubt.

"Of course," Crew said, standing and offering her his hand. She shook it, took his card even as my husband did the same for Detective Prouse. "If you need anything from us, we're here to assist, though I know you have your own case well in hand."

The detective nodded, tucking Crew's card away. "Never hurts to have a second set of eyes, especially your caliber." It could have gone badly, I knew that. Not every detective had a soft spot for the FBI. Fortunately, this one seemed amenable to my husband's prior career choices. He nodded to me then. "No more sneaking around, you two."

Crew pressed his right hand to his heart. "No more need, detective," he said.

The door opened, Norma's distress at Che Mantegna pushing past her lost when her apology to Phyllis for the interruption was cut off by the doctor's aggressive confrontation.

"What's going on?" He glanced at me, at Crew. Noted Lauren's presence, the detective, how distraught Phyllis looked. Then glared at us again. "Did you kill Ian?"

I almost snorted. "We certainly didn't," I said. "Nor did we attempt to sabotage a drug trial."

Che flinched. Stared. Blanched so pale I thought he might keel over. Oh, did I fail to mention we didn't tell the detective what we'd overheard? Instead of throwing Che under the bus, I stepped back and let Prouse handle it.

"We need to talk, Dr. Mantegna," the detective said. "About the trial and the possibility it led to Dr. Linder's death."

Che barely made it to the chair I'd just vacated,

sinking down into it with a thud. "Of course," he said, looking up at me, dark eyes settling into dull acceptance.

I left as my phone buzzed, Crew remaining behind, checking my messages in the hall outside the office door. Poor Norma looked frazzled, but there wasn't much I could do except throw her a kind smile as I dialed Daisy.

"Exciting morning," she said.

"You could say that," I laughed. "What have you got?"

"Just some confirmation for you," she said. "I managed to get in touch with one of Taylor Dulle's former coworkers. Sounds like she has a habit of infiltrating herself into teams behind drug trials and convincing them to sign with her company. And, if she can't do that, she creates enough conflict the teams themselves either dissolve or end up falling apart under accusations of fraud and faked research."

"So, it's a trend," I said. "What if Ian Linder found out what she was up to with Che and confronted her about it? Was going to turn her in?"

"Sounds like motive to me," Daisy said.

And yet, I'd honestly believed Taylor when she told Che she wouldn't get her own hands dirty. So, if she didn't do it, did she convince someone under her thumb to? Not Che, not from the conversation they'd had just a few hours ago. Then who?

Lauren?

Hmmm.

"Oh, one more thing," Daisy said. "Kit

uncovered something about Phyllis Haines." Keys clicked in the background as Kit's cheerful voice said, "Hi, Fee! Did you get arrested?"

"Crew sweet-talked us out of that," I said. "What did you find?"

"Your clinic administrator has been a naughty girl," Kit said. "And has terrible luck. At least, if the financial difficulties she's in thanks to her gambling habit say anything about it." Well now, that was interesting. "Could be why she's in cahoots with Nero Parson." Kit giggled. "I love that word. *Cahoots.*"

"See if you can tie her to him any other way," I said. "Personal relationship, whatever. How they met, even. If they have a connection, we can use that as evidence." No, she wasn't part of the case I'd been hired to work, but if she was selling drugs to the black market through her clinic, drugs that were meant for those who trusted her, you bet your britches I'd be doing everything I could to bring her down.

"On it, boss." Kit's voice faded even as she spoke, Daisy's returning.

"Liz is still looking into that paperwork you sent us," my bestie said, "but from what both of us could uncover, this isn't the first time she's handed over evidence like that to authorities. And not always with the most accurate results."

I was hardly surprised. "Stay on it and keep me up to date," I said.

"Of course," she said, Queen Efficiency making

me grin. "Anything else I can do for you right now?" She stopped typing.

"I'll be in touch," I said. Caught movement out of the corner of my eye and looked up, spotting Brooke Parlor hovering nearby, cheeks pink and face a mask of anxiety. "Actually, yes. Look into Brooke Poplar," I said before hanging up and approaching the nurse. Because I only then wondered just what it was she'd been doing in Dr. Linder's office herself.

One last message landed before I could chat with the nurse. This one was from Penny.

David came through, she sent. *Two of the pills you gave him were a match to one another. A and C.* They were, in order, the one I'd taken from Dr. Linder's mouth and the half a pill Lloyd gave me. *It'll take him a while to break down the full composition.*

No need, I sent back. *And the third?*

The one you marked B was totally different, she sent, *and had very little, if any, medicinal value.*

So, Taylor's pills were a hoax. The ones she supplied to Lauren would paint Linder with a fraudulent brush. With the suggestion Daisy just handed me this wasn't the first time Taylor forged fake documents, I was fairly confident the drug rep was purposely creating evidence to suit her ends. But if the two pills I sent in were real and hers wasn't, where did she get the fake meds?

Thanks, Penny, I sent. *And thank David for me.*

I now owe him dinner, she sent. *Apparently, putting his job at risk was bigger than his IOU. A date it is.*

Sorry about that, I sent.

All good. Worth it. Hug the Stocks for me.

I certainly would. And turned to do just that, forgetting about the young woman waiting to talk to me. She hadn't forgotten about me, though. Brooke almost pounced on me when I strode past her, grasping my hand, apology stuttering out before I could stop her. "I'm so sorry, I had no idea, you're the good guys!" She shook her head, high ponytail shivering with the motion. "I didn't mean to blow your cover, but I didn't know what else to do."

"You suspected us all along," I said.

Brooke shrugged, dimpling. "There was just something off," she said. "And you seemed to have trouble remembering your husband's name."

Ah, my bad. "I usually work alone," I said. "This undercover stuff isn't my forte."

She bobbed an eager nod, sighing deeply. "Again, I'm so sorry. Things have been just awful lately, and I thought I was doing the right thing."

"Awful?" I motioned for her to join me, took a seat in one of the chairs lining the wall of the corridor. She sat with me, swallowing hard, looking back over her shoulder at where Norma had retreated to the desk in the lobby.

"Dr. Linder wasn't the nicest man," Brooke said, leaning in, big eyes blinking tears. "He was terrible to the patients, only cared about his trial. But he was worse with us." She wiped at the tears now trickling down her cheeks. "He did everything he could to make our lives miserable." Her small hands wrung in her lap. "If he finds anything out about you at all, he blackmails you with it."

Ah, so that was it. "I have to ask you why you were in his office last night," I said. "Somewhere you had no reason to be."

She nodded immediately. "I know," she said. "I shouldn't have gone in there. It's just..." Brooke finally let out a long and shaking breath, "he had something he was holding against me, and I couldn't let it ruin my career if he was gone."

CHAPTER TWENTY-ONE

I DIDN'T SAY ANYTHING, letting her share the details, knowing silence was the best motivator for others to speak. Brooke didn't seem reluctant anyway, even eager to share her story.

She dashed the tears from her face. "I swear, it wasn't my fault, but he made it look like it was." Brooke's voice broke. "And it's not just me, either. He keeps files on the staff. Knows things about us, holds secrets against us."

"What happened?" The poor thing. Yeah, I was feeling for her, because I'd barely had any interaction with Linder, and I couldn't stand the man. Being under his thumb? No thanks.

"He said I mixed up medications between two of his patients." She whispered that truth like it hurt her to the core. "But I didn't, I swear." She clutched at me then, earnest and shaking. "I gave them what he told me to, what was on their charts. But when I went back and checked, the charts were switched, and my signature was on both." Brooke kicked at the carpet with the toe of one white sneaker, jaw jumping, eyes blazing with sudden rage. "He set me up, I know it." She sagged back then, anger draining out of her. "I think he made a mistake, realized it and tried to cover it up. But I don't have any proof and he kept the evidence. That's the thing, though," she said, energy renewed. "Why I know it wasn't me who messed up the meds. Why not get me fired? Push the issue? Why hold it over my head?" She glanced around again. "You know Henry Giles? The orderly?" I nodded, I certainly did. Liked him, for what that was worth. "He has a record and Dr. Linder found out. Tried to use it to get him fired." She shook her head, face pinched. "It didn't work, but Phyllis is upset. That means one mistake and his job could be gone like *that*. Poof." She snapped her fingers.

Henry had a record? Likely nothing to concern me, but a loose end to tie up. Besides, Brooke had a point. And clearly an investigative streak of her own. "So, you were looking for the charts," I said.

Brooke nodded with visible misery, letting my hand go and slumping, lips in a wry twist. "I was so surprised to find you there I panicked."

Fair enough. "Thanks for being honest," I said. "If I find what you're looking for, I'll let you know."

Brooke's look of utter relief had me smiling. She bounced to her feet and hugged me when I joined her, before backing off with a rueful grin.

"Sorry," she said. "Thank you!" And hurried off while I watched her go, mystery solved.

"Something I should know?" Crew had joined me without me noticing, the sound of voices from the office becoming rather heated. He seemed calm enough, however, that I trusted the angry exchange inside wasn't about us.

I told him about Phyllis and then Brooke's situation, my husband back to the man I loved so much, listening carefully without interrupting until I was done.

"We need to confront Phyllis," Crew said. Looked up as Detective Prouse strode past with a nod for both of us, Lauren following him, head down. "If the drug really does work, it could be worth millions."

"Billions." Che Mantegna paused next to us, looking weary and resolved. "Come with me." We followed him as he strode down the corridor, this time turning down a hall we hadn't used before. I was surprised to find a lab at the end, now annoyed with myself that I hadn't thought to check for one. Because of course, all the up-to-date data would be stored in this bright, white room filled with testing equipment and a computer with a woman's smiling face on the home screen.

"My wife," Che said, soft and sad, before sitting down. "Let's have a look." He scrolled through to a new screen, using a login and password to access another, though it was obvious to me he'd managed to somehow lift the dead man's information because the page welcomed him as Dr. Ian Linder. "My god," Che whispered. "It's true." He scrolled through page after page of data that made no sense to me, the names of patients flickering past before Che sat back and swiveled on his stool to meet our gazes with his own filled with shock. "It's true," he said, bemused, awed. "It's working." That dazed joy turned to fear and then sullen anger as his gaze dropped to the floor. "It's working."

"Which means your arrangement with Taylor is jeopardizing the health of everyone in the trial," I said, "and all of the others who might benefit from it."

Che looked up again, guilt in him, and old hurt so powerful it made me uncomfortable. "I hadn't done anything yet," he said. Ran one hand over his face. "Thank goodness. I only agreed to help Taylor because Lauren Sigler was here. I thought she had good reason. But Taylor did this, didn't she? She lured Lauren here and set me up to ruin the trial." Che choked then, sobbed once, hands trembling as they ran through his dark hair. "I can't believe I almost destroyed her legacy."

"Your wife," I said as gently and kindly as I could.

"Yes," Che said, coughing softly to clear his throat. "Margaretta would have been forty-five yesterday." His face collapsed, body sagging, emotion draining out of him and leaving him empty. "I blamed Ian, you know. For her death. But it was my fault. My drug. I created it. When she died, I backed away, let Ian take over. He turned me into little more than an assistant and it was *my* drug." Che's fists thudded against his thighs once, rage revealing itself before it melted away again in a flash. "But it wasn't Ian. It was me. My fault. She died because I put her in the trial. She must have been getting the placebo." Che wailed softly, a horrible, broken sound, turning toward the computer again. "I ended the trial early. I could have saved those people. It's all on me. Ian, it's all on *me*." He broke down into weeping, both hands covering his face, while Crew stepped back and nodded to me. Which was my signal to move in.

I did, not just out of duty, but compassion, one hand settling on Che's shoulder. "Why was he kicking you out of the trial? Did he find out you were working with Taylor?"

"No," Che said, pulling himself together enough to speak. "He knew I didn't have faith in the drug, but he couldn't run the trial without me because my name is on the patent application. But he said he found a way to have me removed and was going to. I don't know how." He shook his head then. "I didn't care. I just wanted him to stop. And to pay for what I thought he did."

I had some knowledge and experience with patents, so his news had me wondering. "We'll look into it," I said. "I'm so sorry. Che, I have to ask."

"I didn't kill him," the doctor said. "I have no

idea who did. I did see him that night. We fought over the whole mess. Lauren was with me." He shrugged. "I left before she did. She was pretty upset too." He looked up at me, blinked. "She was furious."

"Understood," I said.

"I have to carry on the trial." Che surged to his feet, wiping at his tears, sudden awakening of passion flushing his face to pink as he slipped past me toward the locked refrigerated cabinet. "If this does work out, imagine." His grin split his face, gratitude awash over him before grim determination returned. "Please, you have to convince Phyllis to let it continue. And to find a way to stop Taylor from interfering."

"Can she?" I glanced at Crew. "What does she have on you?"

Che hesitated then. "Recorded conversations," he admitted. "Emails in which I agree to interfere."

"Did you ever follow through?" Crew's question had the doctor frowning.

"No, not yet," he said. "She was going to supply me with replacement drugs to swap out for the real thing." Which meant, the one I'd stolen from Lauren had to be from that batch. Proof against Taylor, not Che.

"Then she has nothing," my husband said. "Carry on. Let us deal with Taylor Dulle."

Che didn't move, staring at Crew in surprise.

"Conspiracy to commit is a crime," my husband said. "But unless she can prove follow through, they're just emails and conversations, Che. Go cure cancer."

The tall doctor laughed suddenly and surged forward to hug Crew who chuckled back when Che let him go.

A happy ending, at least in part. How rare. Except Che wasn't done. He settled somewhat and hesitated before telling us the last piece of the puzzle in his possession.

"I have no idea if it means anything or not," he said, "but I've always wondered about Sandra."

"Linder?" I felt my instincts wake and buzz in response. "What do you mean?"

"It's her tests." He shrugged. "Every time I've done a dive into her bloodwork, I come up confused. I'd show you, but it won't make sense to you." He gestured at the computer. "Thing is, it's always different. Like completely different. White counts off, markers all over the place." Che stopped again before blurting the last. "I don't think the blood samples are hers."

Which only sealed the deal on what I'd been thinking, pondering since our conversation in the garden, if only subconsciously. It surfaced now as Che revealed what I guess I suspected all along.

"She's not really sick," I said.

Che hesitated. "Why pretend?"

I knew exactly why. And it was motive for murder.

CHAPTER TWENTY-TWO

"ALL DONE WITH THE trial?" I interrupted Sandra's sneaking exodus as she tried to slip out the side door of the building. And no, I hadn't somehow become psychic or anything. The moment I realized the truth, I hoofed it to the residential area, saw Sandra packing her things, and circled around as she exited her room. The fact she took the left instead of the right meant she wasn't aiming for the foyer, was she? I made it to the pathway outside the side door just in time.

Sandra squealed at the sight of me, dropping her bags, one of them spilling sideways over the flagstones. A stack of files tumbled out, scattering over the ground, Linder's wife falling to her knees to gather them up.

Too late. It wasn't hard to make out the names on the tabs, the fact she was in possession of files on patients of the clinic. How did I know? Because Bernice Aberstock's was right there at the toes of my shoes where it had skidded to a halt.

"I know why you faked your illness," I said as Crew and Detective Prouse arrived, Che on their heels, Phyllis huffing her way to join us while Sandra gained her feet, scowling at me. "But what did you think you would accomplish with all this?" I gestured at the scattered files now fluttering in the breeze.

She didn't answer. Didn't have to. Because just as I finished speaking, Taylor Dulle came hurrying around the corner, head down over her phone, looking up just before she reached us. Her whole body jerked to a halt, a frozen statue of shock and horror lasting just long enough for her agile mind to make out the fact she was caught before she spun and tried to run.

I almost chased her. Was too slow on the uptake. Instead, my handsome and very fast husband did the job. And though he was athletic and much taller than her, she impressed me. Taylor actually made it about twenty feet at a full sprint in heels before Crew managed to catch her.

"It's not fair!" Sandra's echoing wail held far more fury than grief. She threw herself down again, trying to gather the files to her as they resisted, slipping and sliding over each other, shedding pages into the breeze that carried them away. "Why couldn't he just love me?"

"This is insane. Sandra." Che spluttered as he made an effort to reclaim the pages, stuffing the files back into the bag she'd used. "What did you think you'd accomplish?"

She snarled at him then, slapping him across the face when he bent too close. Che retreated in shock while Sandra collapsed utterly, fists pounding the pavement.

"If he wouldn't love me, I was going to ruin him." She pointed at Taylor as, now protesting and jerking against Crew's grasp, the drug rep tried to escape. "This is all your fault."

"I have no idea what you're talking about." Taylor had clearly come up with some kind of cover story in the moments it had taken Crew to catch her.

"Then why run?" My husband's cool logic was a force to be reckoned with.

"These two," Taylor said, pointing at Sandra and Che, "have been conspiring to sabotage the trial. They both threatened me. I knew if you caught them, I'd be on the block. But I didn't do anything wrong."

Wow, she really thought that would work? "Sandra," I said, ignoring Taylor for the moment, "did you kill your husband?"

She snorted like that amused her, though there was enough bitterness in it, a level of authentic resentment I had to believe her. "I wish," she snarled. "Yes, I was there last night. In his office. I just wanted him to finally see me." That kind of pathetic had me wincing internally but unable to look away. "He told me he knew I'd lied, faked my tests.

He was going to divorce me." She wailed out that last little bit. "I was so angry, I left." She shook her head. "I know, it's a motive. But I loved him. I couldn't kill him, not even then." Her grieving widow snapped in an instant to madwoman as she met my eyes. "I'm *glad* he's dead." She cackled a laugh before falling over onto her side, weeping all over again.

Wow. My emotional rollercoaster had nothing on her.

"You see?" Taylor's desperate grasping only made me eye roll. "She's crazy. You can't believe a word she says."

"It's over, Taylor," Che said, turning with weary resignation to Phyllis. "She's right about me, though. I was going to help her sabotage the trial."

"This is outrageous." Why did Phyllis look so vindicated? Oh, you bet I was calling her on that in a moment. "Detective, arrest all of them." She waved one hand in the general direction of the trio in question. "How dare you all betray me and the clinic like this? Our patients?"

"You might want to pull back on the accusations there, Ms. Haines," I said, Crew's amusement at my dry tone just between us as he flashed me the barest grin. Yeah, he loved this part too, apparently. "Considering we have evidence of your association with Nero Parson and Parson BioChem. That you've been illegally routing prescription drugs to the black market to cover your gambling debts." Okay, so I didn't have solid evidence yet, but the video was enough to get the ball rolling if the detective asked and I had faith Daisy and Kit would find what I needed. "Not to mention Ian threatened to leave, didn't he?" I recalled the conversation I'd overheard between them, the heat of the moment doing its job, like it always seemed to, connecting the dots. "He was going to pull the trial from your clinic."

Again, I was shy on proof, but it didn't matter anyway. Phyllis gulped, looked around at everyone while I finished what I started, including the two uniformed officers who now joined us, and caved into her own weeping mess.

"You're right," she sobbed. "He was going to leave me." She glanced in panicked focus at all of us, as though seeking support, commiseration, some kind of compassion, and found nothing of the sort. "He wanted to take the trial elsewhere. I knew it was working, I couldn't let him just leave." She gasped, both hands covering her mouth. As if she just realized she gave her own motive for murder. "I didn't kill anyone, I swear! If Ian left, I'd lose out on millions."

There was that. But the detective didn't seem to care one way or the other.

"I think we have enough handcuffs for everyone," Prouse said in his own dry voice. "Let's get this sorted out downtown, shall we?"

I'd just wrangled murder, theft, sabotage and drug trafficking. How was your week going?

CHAPTER TWENTY-THREE

BERNICE HUGGED ME FOR the third time, her tears welcome when paired with the beaming smile on her face. Lloyd's round cheeks were also wet, tracking into his full, white beard, the pair of them overwhelmed to the point they could barely speak while I found myself tearing up all over again.

"Remission?" Bernice laughed out loud, hugging her husband this time, as she absorbed the truth. "Really?"

"The trial worked?" Lloyd seemed utterly floored by that.

"You owe your brother an apology," she said, gently patting his cheek.

He let out a breath and kissed her soundly. "I do

at that. And more than that. Bernie, you're going to be okay."

"Of course, my darling," she said, arms around his neck. "I have you."

Okay, enough, or I'd been on the floor sobbing like a little kid.

We finally filled them both in on everything we knew, and it was a lot, Detective Prouse wasting no time and kindly giving us the details to share when he was done.

"Dr. Mantegna is off the hook," Crew said as the Aberstocks sat us down in their room, Bernice holding his hands as he leaned in toward her. "There was no proof of action taken, just intent, so I was able to convince the detective to hold off. He agreed and is going to talk to the prosecutor in Che's favor."

"Which means the trial gets to keep going," I said, smiling at both Aberstocks. "Lauren Sigler agreed to approve it and stay on to supervise so there's no doubt whatsoever moving forward."

"Why didn't Ian tell us Bernice was in remission?" Lloyd's troubled expression had me patting his knee in understanding.

"According to Che, the most recent batch of tests didn't get processed until after the murder," I said. "Literally this morning. While he might have suspected, Dr. Linder didn't know."

"You said there was a question about the patent." Poor Lloyd had been on the dark side for too long. He struggled to accept the all's well that ends well he'd been presented, and I couldn't blame him for that.

"I had a friend in the business look into it." My call to Nicole Powell had garnered instant assistance, the former inventor I'd met turned investigator for the patent office eager to help. While we hadn't really stayed in touch since I met her and her daughter, Callie, during the convention in Reading—was that really my very first case? It felt like an age ago—I knew Nicole had chosen to do her best to protect inventors like herself and Callie the best way she knew how—from inside the machine that safeguarded creators.

I obviously still had brownie points built up with her because she prioritized my request and got right back to me. "Turns out Dr. Linder was trying to falsify a new patent claiming different ingredients. But according to Che, none of what Linder was claiming was enough to warrant a new patent. All it would have done would be muddy the process and lock the claim up in court."

"Which would give Linder enough time to wrap up this trial without Che," Crew said. "And, with what he already suspected—that the drug was working—on his side, he'd have the financial means to fight Che after the fact."

"Taylor took advantage of the confusion to falsify records," I said, only hearing the truth from Liz a few minutes prior, but happy to have the truth to share. "Not that she'll get away with it." I hoped.

"Linder was going to be a billionaire," Lloyd said.

"And profit off the ill and desperate," I said. "He

was already in talks with several pharmaceutical companies, none of which were Taylor's." That had to have pissed her off. To the point she'd kill him? The pills stuffed in his mouth was a clear anger move. Or a distraction from the real killer?

Didn't matter. Not my problem anymore. I'd finally let that go because the Aberstocks took priority and whoever did murder Dr. Linder was Detective Prouse's problem now.

So, maybe Crew was right after all.

Shh. Don't tell him I said so.

We left them to celebrate privately, heading back to our room to pack. I was so ready to get out of there, I didn't even think about our cover story. We'd just entered our room when a knock came, Brooke Poplar smiling at us from the other side, no longer helping herself to our space.

"Dr. Mantegna would like to see you both in the clinic," she said. "He has the results of your testing and wanted to deliver them personally."

Our…?

Oh, dear.

I glanced at Crew who hesitated too. Then shrugged, arm around my shoulders, gentle smile sweet and adorable.

"Do you want to know?" He left that question hanging while I pondered it.

"I guess I do," I said. "Let's go."

Brooke led the way, pausing outside the door to the office to grasp my wrist and smile at me. "I'm moving on," she said. "Leaving the clinic, off to a new adventure. I just wanted to say goodbye."

"Take care of yourself," I said. "I hope everything works out."

She waved over her shoulder, bouncing off, while I entered the office with more trepidation than maybe I should have felt.

Only to see Che's beaming face, shaking his hand with returned enthusiasm as he guided me to sit with him and Crew on the sofa under his window. His office wasn't the austere and overbearing space Dr. Linder's had been, instead a welcoming and comfortable place to lounge with a standing desk tucked away in one corner and the filing cabinets all polished wood that looked more esthetic than functional.

"I realize your visit was just a front," Che said, "but I wanted to share what we learned anyway." I nodded, taking Crew's hand, my husband squeezing ever-so-gently. "From what we can tell, you're both in excellent health. There's absolutely no reason we could find for you not to get pregnant." He frowned a little then as my whole body unclenched. "That being said, have you been trying?"

I shook my head, Crew too. While hesitant about that denial because, again, I hadn't *not* been.

"So, this wasn't about a real issue?" Che sat back again, smiling. "Excellent. Well, from my perspective, you're good to go. Though, and don't take this wrong, Fiona," he nodded to me, "if you are going to start, you're still in a safe window. But you're nearing thirty-five. So, if you're planning a family, you may want to think about sooner rather than later."

We left his office and returned to our room, my body feeling a little like goo, the release of tension I didn't know I'd been clinging to leaving me wobbly and emotional all over again.

Packing happened fast, Crew on his way out the door with our bags before I realized I'd somehow misplaced my favorite bracelet. I let him go, doing a deep dive into the sofa, under the bed and in the bathroom, frustrated when the adorable pug charm jewelry he'd bought me for Christmas didn't turn up.

I'd been through a similar situation in January, though the loss of the bangle wasn't accidental. The moment that thought crossed my mind, I caught my breath. Stopped in my tracks. And replayed a conversation I'd overheard between Phyllis Haines and Norma at reception the day I arrived.

My phone vibrated in my pocket, drawing my attention, as did the text from Kit Somersby.

I connected the dots between Phyllis and Nero Parson, she sent. *Fired off the info to the detective already, so that's sorted. Oh, and in case you were wondering, selling black-market drugs is a huge industry.* I was aware. I'd been down that road before, shared a wedding anniversary with the research behind it, in fact. Good times. *Turns out Phyllis's ex-husband was the connection to Nero Parson. They were old friends.* Nice to have that piece of the bow tied. *One last thing flagged, not sure if this is helpful,* she sent, *but one of the staff there has an old record for shoplifting.*

Record? Oh, right. Brooke mentioned the orderly, Henry Giles, was an ex-con. I hadn't chased it down, hadn't had time. Felt unrelated despite the fact if Brooke was right, Ian Linder had almost cost Henry his job. I nearly disregarded the rest of the text. Until it registered what she wrote. Shoplifting. Wait, theft? That connected the dots for me and had me fuming. But, before I could storm off and accuse Henry of stealing my bracelet (and who knew what else), Kit shared the name of the person in question.

With no idea how helpful she'd been.

Thanks, Kit, I sent. *Great job. I think you just caught a murderer.*

I was on the move and out the door before she answered, but I knew that would make her day.

It didn't take much to convince Norma to let me back into Dr. Linder's office, nor to give me his username and password to access his desktop email. And, in turn, it didn't take long to find what I'd been looking for, the message addressed to Phyllis still in drafts but clearly ready to be sent. With the details of the contents completing my intuitive guesswork, I forwarded the message to Detective Prouse with a note that he had one more set of handcuffs to use before storming out of the office in pursuit of my bracelet.

I found the thief emptying her locker, Brooke Poplar dumping her things rapidly into a backpack, the rattle of a small, plastic box suspect as she yelped and turned when I grabbed the strap of her bag.

"Let's just have a look, shall we?" I dumped the backpack out onto the bench in front of the row of lockers, the box landing hard and cracking open, contents spilling over to tinkle on the floor as the collection of personal jewelry she'd stolen from patients emptied out of the hiding place. I retrieved my pug bracelet and dangled it in front of her, Brooke's flat and angry expression a far cry from the young, eager nurse I thought I'd come to know. "Well played," I said. "You almost had me. But taking this?" I tucked the beloved bangle into my pocket. "Big mistake, Brooke."

"I never knew when enough was enough," she admitted without a hint of guilt, glancing past me at the exit. What, ready to run? Let her try. "Whatever. Call the cops. I'll get a slap on the wrist."

"They tend to throw murderers into prison for life," I said.

Brooke flinched, flat and angry stare then flickering to an attempt at innocence before she let out a big sigh and tossed her hands, more annoyed than afraid. "Fine, yes, I strangled the old jerk." Okay, she used stronger language than that, but I'll spare you the details. "He found out I was helping myself to things and was going to tell Phyllis." She shrugged then, all casual and unconcerned. And I thought Taylor was a slice of delight. This kid's lack of empathy had my skin crawling. "He wouldn't listen. Wasn't interested in negotiating, either." She wriggled her hips then giggled. The implication? Just gross. "So, I choked him with his laptop cord." Brooke barked a laugh. "I figured they'd pin it on that crazy-ass wife of his. Or Taylor. Whichever. Didn't matter to me."

"That's why you stuffed his mouth with the drugs from the trial to distract investigators," I said.

Brooke winked. "I'd been stockpiling them. That's how he knew I was stealing. When I found out Taylor was trying to sabotage the trial, I figured why not?" Again with the glance past me. What was she looking at? I refused to be distracted. "Besides, everyone in this place was on the take. Phyllis, too."

"Nurses see everything," I said.

She winked. And, for the third time, looked over my shoulder. As her eyes suddenly widened in shock. "Look out!"

I turned. Listen, don't judge me. I know she was playing me. I knew it the instant I reacted to her feint. There wasn't anyone there. But try telling that to my instincts and sense of self-preservation after almost dying more times than I cared to admit. So, I turned. To nothing emptiness, no threat, just as Brooke lunged for me, something shiny in her hand.

The needle hurt when she dug it into my arm, thumb depressing the plunger. Brooke pushed back, grabbing her bag, kicking at me as my body betrayed me, numbness sweeping through me in a wave so powerful I staggered and almost went down.

No way was I letting her win. Not this little fluff of nothing, after everything I'd been through. I was Fiona Fleming, and she was nothing.

So there.

With the final bit of my control remaining, and not much else to call on, I threw myself at her departing back with the stubbornness Bernice

Aberstock admired my last resort, crashing into Brooke and carrying us both to the ground as someone shouted.

She cried out, of course, she did, tried to play the victim. To the wrong person, thankfully. Because as she did, the door to the locker room opened and Crew ran in, his face my final view before the world went black.

He'd take care of things, I had no doubt. While I dipped into darkness without further struggle. I was safe. Crew had my back. And yet.

Unconscious again. Awesome (in the most sarcastic way possible).

CHAPTER TWENTY-FOUR

THE DELICIOUS SCENT OF chocolate chip cookies filled my kitchen, two trays already cooling on racks while the rest of the batch finished browning as the timer counted down. I wiped off the counter and removed my apron as March sunshine poured in through the windows, my playlist luring a few dance steps out of me while the buzzer dinged its announcement my creations were ready. Petunia chuffed at me, white rims showing around her dark eyes, a soft bark of appeal making me laugh.

"These aren't for you, sweet girl," I said.

Crew trotted down the back stairs to join me, setting aside his tablet to land a lovely kiss on my lips before helping himself to a cookie. The sight of him had my stomach fluttering, but not just out of love. Nerves had me almost fumbling the last tray of cookies, I admit it, while he didn't seem to notice. "You're trying to give Lucy a run for her money," he said, taking a seat at the island to enjoy the treat while I discarded my oven mitts and leaned into the counter with my own cookie to enjoy.

Oh, you better believe my fat pug begged for a corner. Which she got, minus the chocolate part, from one of my shaking hands. "I promised Mom I'd contribute something to her bake sale thingie for the high school," I said. Smacked his fingers when he tried for another cookie. "For the kids, Crew."

He winked and snagged one anyway. "They don't need the sugar," he said.

Bratty husband. And best in the world. Who saved me, I was positive of that, when Brooke overdosed me on stolen sedative—enough to bring down a horse, according to Dr. Aberstock—and planned to leave me to die. All but for Kit's text sharing the same information with him as she did with me and Crew's unerring knowledge of my brain's inner workings.

He came looking for me. Just in the nick of time.

"I heard back from Detective Prouse," Crew said, munching the cookie he'd stolen. Petunia had shifted herself to his immediate vicinity in the hope of crumbs, only to be rewarded with her own chocolate-free corner from his hands. "Brooke Poplar has quite a rap sheet, and not just in Rhode Island. Turns out she's wanted for a string of thefts in four states, but the cops didn't put the pieces together." He often complained about lack of intercommunication when it came to law enforcement branches, so I didn't need to hear that song and dance again. "She's got a good lawyer, but thanks to you, she'll be going away for a long time." The prosecution team already asked me to testify and I'd agreed. "And Phyllis Haines plead guilty to diverting drugs from the clinic. But the best part?" He grinned at me as he took another cookie. "Liz is over the moon because it turns out Phyllis was aces at keeping evidence. That means Nero Parson and his fake corp will finally go down, too."

Karma, baby. And a topic of discussion that didn't make my insides gooey with anxiety. "What about Taylor Dulle?" I pulled out the cardboard box flats Mom supplied me with, shoving some toward Crew for folding, as he answered.

"Yeah, that story might not have the happy ending we hoped for." Crew wrangled one of the boxes into shape while I tried to figure out which tabs went where. "Her company's lawyers are all over it. I guess she pulled out liability questions and suggested heavily the fake pills were manufactured by their own labs, so they're defending her. But I can't imagine she'll last much longer after the trial."

Slow burn on fate's payback. Well, it would have to do.

"I guess Sandra Linder tried to take Che to court," Crew said, handing me a box. "She dropped it pretty quick when the patent she had fell apart."

He folded another. "Nicole came through."

I'd have to send her, Teddy and Callie a box of cookies. "Hey, at least she has her health."

Crew snorted. "Lloyd and Bernice are home next week."

"I know." Such amazing news. "Bernice called. Che approved her release, but I guess she's still under his care for the next few months." I could only hope the drug really was the miracle the Aberstocks—and so many others—were hoping for. "Mom suggested a party at The Iris. Do you think it's too soon?"

Crew shook his head, second box built and moving onto the third. "I think it's an awesome idea. We need a win, Fee." He sighed shaking his head. "Reading's been through a lot. Town's so quiet these days." The lingering aftereffects of the O'Shea family invasion would likely hang over us a long time. "Inviting everyone out to celebrate the Aberstocks sounds like the perfect way to kick off on a new beginning."

He was totally right about that.

Crew stood and circled the counter, hands on my hips, turning me toward him. Stirring up the anxiety I'd been fighting all morning. "You know, we didn't get to have that talk."

I knew exactly what he meant, of course, I did. Instead of our planned conversation on our drive home after the case, I'd been distracted by the fact I'd been knocked unconscious, the two of us talking work rather than about the looming question hanging over us ever since.

"Babies?" Crew kissed me gently. "It's hardly now or never, Fee. But what do you think?"

I drew a little breath, tiptoeing up to kiss him softly on the mouth. While my insides did a dance I could barely contain. "We just got ourselves sorted," I said. "The life we want, the jobs we want. This house, our marriage, Reading." I hesitated then, heart fluttering in my chest. And something else fluttering elsewhere. "Are we ready to give that up?"

Crew kissed me deeply in response. "Ready when you are."

"Good to know," I said, finally able to tell him what I'd been holding in for the last few hours. The source of my anxiety and nerves, the reason for my baking, honestly, and need for distraction. Since Che messaged me privately with the results of the final test they'd done and just got around to completing. He apologized, said he hadn't followed through because he'd been busy, the clinic reorganizing and, frankly, he'd put us out of his mind.

Until that test crossed his desk, and he knew he needed to reach out.

See, there was a good reason I'd been so emotional during our time at the clinic, beyond the scope of my normal temperamental nature.

You've guessed already, haven't you? Poor Crew had no idea.

"Why's that?" His soft and sweet smile had me relaxing into the truth.

And then blinking through my tears with an anxious and happy laugh. "Turns out you're going to be a daddy," I said, "so your ready and willingness is the kind of news I wanted to hear."

He froze. Made me giggle nervously all over again.

Before the giant whoop I know they heard to town square preceded my amazing husband lifting me into the air and swinging me around while Petunia barked her excitement at his happy response.

We were going to be parents.

Oh, dear.

Looking for more Fiona Fleming? Coming soon from **Fleming Investigations Cozy Mysteries**

#9 Haute Couture and Death

While you wait for more Fiona Fleming, why not come along for another investigation? Check out chapter one of my newest series, **Finders Keepers:** *The Curse in the Carousel Horse.*

PATTI LARSEN

THE CURSE
IN THE CAROUSEL
HORSE

FINDERS KEEPERS COZY MYSTERIES: ONE

CHAPTER ONE

If you've never been to an auction, you're missing out. I adore them, my favorite thing ever. The meander through the collection of items up for sale while potential bidders whisper and connive and pretend they couldn't care a beat if they win or lose gives a rush like no other. The not-so-subtle build of tension as your item or items of choice near the block only adds to the anticipation. All for the heat of the moment when the caller rapid fires at the gathering and paddles wave-like Fourth of July flags in the stiff breeze of his encouragement. It's as exciting as it gets, let me tell you, and I'm not known to be excitable.

Though my husband Hank might argue that fact.

As for my client, he hovered near me as we

walked the warehouse space where the items up for sale stood on display, as jittery as a newborn colt at his mother's shoulder, dark eyes wide, dabbing at the sweat on his furrowed brow with that ever-present red gingham kerchief of his.

"There it is," Norman Ryanette whispered loudly enough I know they heard him across the Potomac, and that great river was a good two hours away from Richmond. So much for subtle. It was hard not to share his excitement, truth be told, at the sight of our quarry now so close at hand.

"Remember," I said, easing forward with a nod to a familiar face here, a stranger there, "cool and composed." You better believe I played on my barely 5'1" unintimidating self in situations like this one. Being a Southern lady, it wouldn't do to let any rivals know the internal buzz of acquisitive excitement had begun like a long drink of sweet tea on a hot day.

Norman stumbled next to me, his anxious expression not helping matters, and worse when I spotted none other than Arlene Plimpton watching me from her own slow predatory circle of the items. Well, she could take her Northern contempt and haughty airs and eat my dust.

Bless her heart.

"I know you know what you're doing, Sissy," Norman said, anxiety making his voice crack, "but you also know just how much this means to me." He paused, gaze falling fully on the centerpiece of this particular auction, a tremulous smile lighting his face. "Margie is going to be so surprised."

I tucked my hand around his elbow and leaned on him enough to get the much larger man moving again. "You hired Finders Keepers for a reason," I said. "It's taken a year to track it down." I paused then, now side-on to the prize, and admired it a moment myself. "Just a little while longer, and it's yours."

The carousel horse might not have looked like much to the casual observer, but I knew better. This had been my most challenging hunt to date, and despite fifteen years restoring antiques and tracking down pieces for clients, I honestly worried I'd finally met my match. Because this was no ordinary horse, nor could any be substituted for Norman's fiftieth wedding anniversary dreams for his adoring wife. I honestly believe it was the Good Lord's will and my own sheer stubbornness that dropped this horse in my lap just in time for the big day.

The very horse on which he'd proposed to his wife.

I spotted the second item I was bidding on for another client nearby, the bone china set a classic and exactly what Jenny Matheson was looking for. It would be an easy acquisition, no matter if Mrs. Arlene Plimpton scooted herself around the horse to lay claim to the set herself. I let her have her moment of unwarranted triumph, her lack of grace showing her card hand so early in the game and offered her a custom Southern smile before turning that wattage on Norman. Momma taught her baby girl how to get what she wanted, and I was walking out with both today or my name wasn't Sicily Scarlett Sloane.

Time to swoop in ever so casual like and have a looky-loo at the provenance. A swift but thorough read of the documentation—in passing, my dear, only in passing—and I had what I needed.

"It's authentic," I told him, voice low, still smiling as I led him away.

"It's the right horse." He beamed at me, once again wiping the moisture from his forehead and cheeks, swabbing the back of his neck where his white shirt collar pressed to his tanned skin. "I can't believe it. At last."

Found in a warehouse on private property by the children of the owner after their father's death, no less. A miracle, praise the Lord and Halleluiah. And yes, I knew how irreverent it was to call on His name in times of material gain, but I also knew He forgave me my trespasses.

Make no mistake, I hadn't lost my pretty little head enough to forget there were others equally as interested in the horse. Despite its rough appearance, this was a classic and, once restored, would be worth far more than it was now. Which, I gauged from previous auctions, should sit right around twenty thousand. However, as I strolled away, dragging Norman with me, I took note of the competition doing their own inspection.

The tall, handsome man in the dark suit had a creepy air about him, and I caught him grinning at me in between his brazen strides that circled the horse with the steady gaze of someone who knew what he had in front of him. That could be a problem. I had hoped not many would recognize the value of an authentic horse from the turn of the 20th century. If bidding grew heated, Norman might be out far more than the amount I hoped for. Not that he cared, already confirming he was happy to pay what was needed to acquire the piece. It certainly made my job easier.

My, but I did love a bottomless purse.

Still, if he didn't have to pay a ridiculous amount, it would help my reputation further. Which had me leaving him to glide to the man still observing the horse with his hands in his pockets, a wry and rather unlikable smirk on his face.

"You're a collector?" I flashed him my charm and he responded as expected with a tip of his head and a quick up and down look I let him think didn't make my skin crawl.

"Fred Miller." He freed one hand from his pocket long enough to shake mine, though bent over it to kiss the back of my fingers instead. "I'm less a collector and more of a treasure hunter."

"Treasure?" I laughed at that, just this side of breathless, watched him light up at the attention. "My Heavens, what sort of treasure?"

He seemed more than amenable to continuing our conversation, but the hasty arrival of one of the auction house staff curtailed further detail. Instead, I noted the sharp look of concern on the young man's face and took note they had similar enough features they had to be related.

"You shouldn't be here." While the elder's expression didn't change from that arrogant bravado, his younger counterpart didn't carry himself with the same confidence. He met my eyes, his that light hazel that sparkles with green in the right light, nodding to me. "Mrs. Sloane," he said, "nice to see you. Good luck today."

My mind fished for a name, came up with it in a flash of inspiration that left me smiling in relief but hopefully looked only endearing. "Michael," I said, remembering he'd delivered my last two wins to me, introducing himself along the way. Michael Burne. Yes, that was it. "Thank you, dear."

He led Fred Miller away, the pair leaning into one another, Michael's hasty conversation met with a casual shrug from the unphased older man while I watched them go with growing curiosity.

A mystery. How delicious.

As I turned back to rejoin Norman, the skirt of my favorite 50s knee-length navy dress power flaring when I walked, I noticed Michael wasn't the only one who seemed unhappy to find Fred Miller here.

From the steady glare of dislike on Dean Drake's face, either the auction house owner had his own run-ins with the man, or his reputation preceded him. I could only imagine the former.

I had barely taken two steps toward my client when I felt something impact my shoulder, knocking me askew with an unladylike squeak of surprise, the offending gentleman who wasn't apparently as bereft of manners as he was patience. He stormed up to

Dean with ridged shoulders and a raised hand pointing in aggressive demand back behind him, his voice loud enough for everyone in the warehouse to hear.

"You know the horse is mine, Dean," he said, "and it's not for sale."

You can imagine my heart went pitter-pat and not in a good way, even as a second person, at least a bit more polite, followed suit and confronted the auction house owner with a sheaf of papers in her trembling hand.

"Wrong," she said in her shaking voice, "it's mine and I want it. Now."

Like what you read? ***The Curse in the Carousel Horse*** is available now! I also have many more cozy mysteries—both contemporary and paranormal—for you to sink your teeth into, all waiting for you at **https://pattilarsen.com/home**. Thank you for reading!

PATTI LARSEN

MAGIC · MAYHEM · MURDER

AUTHOR NOTES

MY DARLING READER:
Gang. Oh my *goodness*.
Fee is *pregnant*.

I've known about this for a while, and I was delighted when she finally let me type that line. And it means some changes are coming.

Namely, her second series is coming to an end. Four more books are pending, but once they are done, Fee told me she needs to take a break. I understand completely, and I hope you do, too.

Now, a caveat—she hasn't told me she's done. Quite to the contrary. It sounds like there's a third series in her voice coming at some point, but I'm as in the dark as you are, so bear with me while she does what Fee does best and tells me when I need to know.

Such a bratty voice, that Fiona Fleming.

Don't despair! As I said, there are four more books ahead before she wants to take a breather. I'm planning to release one a month (May-August 2022) until they are all out. While taking time off from everything else to update some business things and enjoy my summer.

As soon as I know more, I'll share. I can tell you Daisy has her own series in the wings, so we'll see what the fall brings. But I'm also working on the number of series I've already released, like **Whitewitch Island**, **Masquerade, Inc.** and **Finders**

Keepers, among others. If you haven't had a chance to check in with Georgia, Petal, Becks, Sissy, Pheobe, Abigail and more, I urge you to do so. There's so much fun waiting for you with those voices, I'm excited to hear what you think!

I'm also working on a fantasy series I've been putting off forever, and I understand if you're not a fan of paranormal. But if you are and you're curious, I'm hoping to publish book one of the **Monstrous Magic Chronology**, *An Ordinary Mage*, in the fall. We'll see—Cricket and Lazlo have been very patient with me, so I'm doing my best to tell their story the way they want it to be told.

As always, happy reading and stay safe and healthy out there!

Best,
Patti

ABOUT THE AUTHOR

EVERYTHING YOU NEED TO know about me is in this one statement: I've wanted to be a writer since I was a little girl, and now I'm doing it. How cool is that, being able to follow your dream and make it reality? I've tried everything from university to college, graduating the second with a journalism diploma (I sucked at telling real stories), am an enthusiastic member of an all-girl improv troupe, Side Hustle (if you've never tried it, I highly recommend making things up as you go along as often as possible) and I get to teach and perform with an amazing group of women I adore. I've even been in a Celtic girl band (some of our stuff is on YouTube!) and was an independent filmmaker (go check out the Lovely Witches Club at https://www.lovelywitchesclub.com). My life has been one creative thing after another—all leading me here, to writing books for a living.

Now with multiple series in happy publication, I live on beautiful and magical Prince Edward Island (I know you've heard of Anne of Green Gables) with my multitude of pets.

I love-love-love hearing from you! You can reach me (and I promise I'll message back) at patti@pattilarsen.com. And if you're eager for your next dose of Patti Larsen books (usually about one release a month) come join my mailing list! All the best up and coming, giveaways, contests and, of course, my observations on the world (aren't you just dying to know what I think about everything?) all in one place: http://bit.ly/PattiLarsenEmail.

Last—but not least!—I hope you enjoyed what you read! Your happiness is my happiness. And I'd love to hear just what you thought. A review where you found this book would mean the world to me— reviews feed writers more than you will ever know. So, loved it (or not so much), your honest review would make my day. Thank you!